In the Congo

URS WIDMER

Translated by Donal McLaughlin

T0078701

LONDON NEW YORK CALCUTTA

This publication was supported by a grant from the Goethe-Institut India

swiss arts council

prɔhelvetia

The original English publication of this book was supported
by a grant from Pro Helvetia, Swiss Arts Council

Seagull Books, 2021

Originally published as *Im Kongo* by Urs Widmer
© Diogenes Verlag AG Zurich, 1996. All rights reserved.

First published in English translation by Seagull Books, 2015
English translation © Donal McLaughlin, 2015

ISBN   978 0 8574 2 825 7

British Library Cataloguing-in-Publication Data
A catalogue record for this book is available from the British Library

Typeset by Seagull Books, Calcutta, India
Printed and bound by WordsWorth India, New Delhi, India

In the Congo

Behind the house my father had inhabited all his life and that he was now the last to leave, to be in my care—my mother died years ago and my sisters, both the little one and the big one, have been living with their husbands and children for a long time now—behind this wonderful, now lost-for-ever house was a forest so large that, if you only knew the way, you could walk from the Swiss border to our front door without ever leaving it. Trees, nothing but trees, and no one to see you. Here and there, a meadow with a distant farm—that, yes!—the lights of a sleepy village, a few cows that you would creep past or an abandoned road you would have to cross, crouching; otherwise, nothing but pathless scrub, from the bank of the Rhine to the overgrown-with-knotgrass rear wall of the house.

It was a long way—more than fifty kilometres; the house was, and is, in Witikon, high above the city of Zurich—but walkable for a vigorous man. I walked it. In the summer, the Rhine was a green river. In winter, it was black. In spring, brown and full of ice floes. Over there was Germany. Looking at them, you couldn't tell—back then, I mean—whether those who, in the night of a new moon, rowed across in narrow boats, or jumped across the ice, were coming to murder people or fleeing from being murdered themselves.

The forest rose so steeply at its edge that, climbing a winding path, I'd have to cling to roots and branches. I was a child and could barely grip my handholds. When it rained, flash floods would race past the house. But the sun was always shining! The forest always shone. Cuckoos would call, other birds too—blackbirds, orioles, goldfinches.

A nightingale sang. If I opened the back door and took a *single* step, I would find myself among sky-high tree trunks. Some were so entwined with ivy, they suffocated and were held upright, dead, until—in a storm perhaps—they'd lean to the side and crash down among wild vines, blackberries and thistles. Sounds would lure me, something squawking, crackling, howling. Three or four steps uphill, and I could no longer see the house. Old legends—or at least the family variety of them—had it that many people, children above all, had wandered, lost, for days and years through the eternal forest until, exhausted, they couldn't continue any further and themselves became trees. Some of the tree-giants had once been someone like me. Pipsqueaks hopping along. Nonetheless, I forced my way through thickets, singing and shuffling through anemones. A groove, when I looked back, through the white blossoms. Animals rustled in the greenery, mice perhaps, or weasels. On the stones at the edge of the forest—lizards. In a clearing only I knew lived dwarfs, or gnomes, they danced, and their chief brought me presents—charms I used to turn myself into a giant whose head towered over the highest treetops. They sang such terrifying songs, anyone who heard them shuddered—except me, for I'd invented these chants.

Somewhere, hidden by a tree, my mother was calling me and, unable to see her, I groped my way towards her voice, tripped over a root and rumbled downhill. I yelled, but the forest floor smelt so cool, I kept my nose in the moss. Of course, she comforted me. 'So, are you all right again, my hero?' My mother did nothing without me. I ran behind her, down the steep path. The dog was somewhere too. 'When will there be something to eat?' Without turning, she replied, 'Soon, my dearest. Soon.' I swept into the house where my big sister, my little sister and my father were at the table. Herr Harder, the gardener, was too. We ate.

*

I grew up and gave up hope of ever seeing a forest like that again. The one I'd known had shrunk, become commercial timberland, full of forest roads. Always and everywhere the segment saws. The noise of the cars. And yet! I'm now among trees again, an infinite number of them, and they're more beautiful than back then. Tree-monsters, everywhere I look. Wild vines form curtains the width of a stage. Waterfalls thunder down. Some trees are so enormous that at their crowns, forests of their own run riot. Animals scurry. Others jump from branch to branch. Birds flutter up into the air. Screams are heard.

A year ago, on a grass runway over there, I got out of a plane which had, apart from the pilot, crates full of empty bottles and a few sacks. A sweltering heat! It was high summer as it is now. Perhaps that's why today—the first anniversary!—I've taken into the jungle forest the laptop that actually belongs to the accounts department. A handy little plastic box. I fill the screen with letters and watch how they vanish into the memory of the machine. My text—gone. I, just seconds later, could no longer say what there was. But the machine remembers even typing errors. A display knows, though I've yet to properly begin, that I've saved already 3,986 characters, 4,002 now. An undeniable and overwhelming feeling—gratitude, and more—is telling me that I need to make an enormous effort today, similar to that made by the gods that brought me here. Because today is a kind of commemoration day. I owe it to them. What happened to me doesn't happen to just anyone. To one in a million perhaps, a bullish estimate. Who knows, perhaps it really was my gnomes from back then. You can't see ghosts.—It may, incidentally, absolutely be the case that those who abandoned me here expect me to offer thanks in the way they would have. To write in my blood, on the bark of a tree, by the light of a full moon, or to gouge the text into my skin. People like them have that kind of tradition, and don't have bodies that hurt.—Anyway, I won't eat until I've finished. Three days should suffice. Writing and fasting. If I don't take any breaks—except for a gulp of water and to answer the call of nature—I should manage in seventy-two hours to write my way forward from the distant Back Then to Now. I'm looking forward to the sacred moment—maybe I'm writing all of this only for that moment—when, my fingers unsure, I'll type in the keys that I've reached the end. That my back is hurting and that I'm terribly hungry—and, simultaneously, my back will be hurting and I will be terribly hungry. Memory and life, for the whiff of a precious moment, will be one. After that, it won't actually matter how I finish the text. I'll write *finis operis* under it, or some equivalent. *Cunius Cunii filius fecit*, and, roaring like a lion, I'll make a dash for the bread and the dried meat already hanging, in a jute sack, on a branch over there. Two bottles of beer will await me there too.

What I'll do then, I don't know. Perhaps I'll print out, in the accounts department, what I've saved on the laptop. There's a printer there. Perhaps I'll send the pile of papers to Hansi. Perhaps I'll put the laptop in the fridge, in the freezer compartment, for the generations to come. Or, on each anniversary, I'll read my printed-out confessions, page by page. Drinking a beer as I do. I could also let the pages drift individually down the river, like water lilies. Or set them alight and let them flutter over the treetops in the jungle forest. Firebirds.

*

It all began on 29 July 1994. A Friday. My father had just come within a whisker of shooting a postman dead, and I was kneeling on the floor of a room in the old people's home in Fluntern—another district in Zurich, ten minutes by car from Witikon—and saying to Herr Berger, only to keep our slow-moving conversation going, 'I am now fifty-six, Herr Berger. I've been working here since I was thirty-one. I'm the best carer in the place. No one can pull the wool over my eyes, not even Sister Anne. And look what I'm doing!'

I was busy using a kitchen knife to remove all the chewing gum that Frau Schroth, the resident whose room it was, had spat and stamped on the floor over the last twenty years. Frau Schroth had died the evening before, at the age of ninety-nine. I was actually a carer in the home—the senior carer!—and not the caretaker, but I couldn't hand the room over to a new resident in this state. The cleaners, two student temps from the USA, had swept the dirt of two decades away in barely fifteen minutes, using so many chemicals you'd have thought they wanted to defoliate Vietnam a second time, and Sister Anne had accepted the room as it was without a moment's hesitation—despite the stains that made the green lino flooring look like a field of flowers in May.

Normally, I wouldn't have cared about all the chewing gum; but my father, my own father, was supposed to move into this room this particular evening. Because he shot the postman. The days of having the house by the forest were over. Whether or not he wanted to, he was about to spend the rest of his life with me, with a geriatric nurse who was his son. He was eighty-one now. Up until a few weeks ago, everything had been going well—with him alone in the lonely house, where, once a week, a woman working for Pro Senectute checked if everything was in order—but he'd then started falling down the stairs and boarding the wrong trams. He refused to strap on an alarm, barely the size of a cigarette packet, with which, as long as he was conscious, he could call for help in any situation, however unpleasant. He'd only have to press a button and a beep would go off in my jacket pocket. On one occasion, he did so—I was in the process of giving Frau Schroth her vitamin tablets—and, trembling with fear, I raced like a madman to Witikon, thundered up the steep garden path, rang and rang the bell and was just lifting an axe to smash the door—when it opened and there was my father, standing before me with a bag of rubbish in his hand. He hadn't heard me and was now staring at the axe hovering over him. Turned out, the alarm was on the kitchen table, under a potful of potatoes pressing on the button.

That he was coming here this very evening, however—that he *had* to come, was to do with the nearly dead postman. That Friday morning, my father had been busy cleaning his service pistol, a monster from the Second World War that, for some reason, hadn't found its way back to the arsenal after demobilization. This cleaning was a mysterious ritual to which he subjected himself every few months. And though the weapon had been unloaded since 8 May 1945, a shot went off and the bullet ended up in a parcel that the postman (who, like any other day, had carted all the post up the stairs for the old gentleman) held. In it was a catskin my father had ordered from a mail-order firm for his rheumatism.

'Oops!' he shouted.

The postman, otherwise a cool lad, was very frightened when he saw the muzzle of the gun pointing at him, right up in front of his chest. He was so shocked, he called the police and they called me; and the solution the head of the local police station in Witikon and I arrived at in the kitchen—my father was at the table with us—was that my father should, with immediate effect, move to my nursing home. Be under my supervision. I called the management of the old people's home and succeeded in getting him moved from 112th on the waiting list to the very top. A gift from the home to their longest-serving employee. The head of the police station, standing next to me, shook my hand, and then my father's, and chose not to press charges of illegal possession of a weapon and attempted murder.

'In this century, even the biggest nincompoop got to run ashore at the Normandy landings or perished in Hiroshima,' I said. 'I'm the only one not to have a fate!'

Herr Berger, who had the room next door, was leaning against the frame of the door, one leg cocked, the other firmly on the ground, and watching what I was doing. I raised my head. 'And my father didn't have one before me.'

'What?'

'A fate.'

'Oh—right.'

'Every morning he took the eight o'clock bus to the office and every night returned so late I was long since asleep. That was the case throughout the war as far as I remember and after the war for sure. He always wore a grey suit and a plain tie. Dark red or blue. In winter, a grey coat. A hat, also grey. Just as, day in day out, I wear these jeans and a T-shirt. I've never experienced anything and never will. Just like my father.'

'Would that be so terrible?' Herr Berger asked. He smiled. He was eighty now. He was wearing, as he always did, a suit made of bright, crude silk which, in the thirties, had no doubt been very expensive but now looked like a spider's web. I, at any rate, through the now-threadbare fabric of the trousers, could see his red boxer shorts in patches. He also wore a panama hat, this too of gossamer, and carried a stick with a rubber ferrule. I got up on my knees. 'Do you have a fate, Herr Berger?'

'I was a merchant,' he said. 'Optical instruments.'

I sighed. A still-hot late-afternoon sun was shining through the window the cleaners had forgotten to clean. Dead flies, dust, a piece of the wing of a moth. Beyond the lake were flashes of summer lightning. A single high cloud in the blue sky. No movement in the air. The sweat was streaming down my face. Herr Berger, too, was fanning himself with one hand.

'Who are you scrubbing so obsessively for?' he asked.

'My father. You'll like him.'

'I survived Frau Schroth,' Herr Berger said. 'He can't be any worse.'

*

(Incidentally, and in parentheses—Sister Anne was my superior, responsible for the first floor. She was strict and firm, that—yes; but she wasn't one of those dragons, like Sister Helga on the second. Rather, she had a gentle voice and was pretty. Breathtakingly beautiful, to tell the truth—not much more than thirty; big, quite a bit bigger than—for example—me. Long blond hair. Round eyes. Everyone, even the oldest residents in the home—especially them!—watched her with their mouths hanging open when she walked along the corridors. There wasn't one who was not in love with her. Even the women were in raptures about her. Once, years ago, I'd gathered up the courage—we, just the two of us, were in the process of making an inventory of the medicines in the medical dispensary—and said, 'Sister Anne. I love you. Will you marry me?' She put a box of 2.5 mg Temesta tablets down on the shelf, turned around slowly and said, 'For that, you can wait until you are black in the face.' We carried on counting as if nothing had happened. Got to the end to discover a vial of morphine was missing, and had to start all over again. It turned out that Anne, I mean, Sister Anne, had it in her hand the whole time.)

*

My father worked for the electric company of the city of Zurich; to this day, I don't know where and as what. His work had something to do with the locks on the Limmat river and the dams in the hinterland of the city. Immediately before the war—this is the one thing I do know—he'd worked out the alarm arrangements that were to save the residents of Zurich if the dam of Lake Sihl broke, back then a spanking new reservoir on the foothills of the Alps. Twenty minutes, he'd calculated, the water frontline would need to roll through the narrow Sihl Valley, drowning cows and farmers on its way to the edge of the city. If the lake was full and emptied completely, the water would be up to people's heads even at Bellevue. So, he fitted the roofs of the houses in the danger zone with sirens that would go off if the safety officer, a farmer living above the dam, pressed a button. The first practice alarm went splendidly, apart from the fact that he'd forgotten to inform the population and triggered a panic. In deadly terror, they ran up the slopes to a predetermined height and, with much wringing of hands, waited for the flood to swallow up their houses.

*

Any such arrangement or practice alarms, it turned out, were of no help to my mother. Nor was the fact that we lived at the uppermost end of Witikon, high above the area subject to flooding. The war was far from over when she died. It was a hot summer's day. I came skipping into the garden—five years of age—and found her lying among the flowers, staring up at the sky. Blood across her throat. Beside her lay Herr Harder, slashed to ribbons. I thought they were sleeping, though, and shook them. The dog was sniffing at the blood. I then ran, screaming, into the house. There was no one there, no father, no other person. I shot for a bit at the toilet door with my bolt rifle. Then I stood on the terrace, unable to take my eyes away from my mother's feet which, far below—naked and white as snow—were sticking out from among the larkspur and hollyhocks on the garden path. The dog, like a statue. Finally, my father came, in an army uniform, oddly. I barely recognized him, this officer with his cap full of golden stripes—who, with his glassy voice, ordered what was a whole troop of men around. They clomped through the leeks with measuring tapes, crushed tomatoes and pumpkins, took photographs with cameras placed on long-legged tripods, and finally carried the two bodies over to a car. My big sister and my little sister were there too by now. The car drove off. My father watched, motionless, with eyes that were stones. Then he took the dog by the collar, lifted it up, then put it down, then went into the house, took off his uniform, sat down at his bench and, without a word, carved puppets all night—a Kasper, a policeman, a crocodile, a princess. Had he sewn the clothes too? At dawn, at any rate, he bent over me— thinking I was sleeping, whispered, 'This one's just for you, Dwarf!' and laid a sorcerer with a long nose and a pointed hat across my chest. Later, he also made a Hitler and a Général Guisan—whose nose broke off when, once, we put on a performance for the children from the village and he tussled with the crocodile.—Soon, my father returned to taking the morning bus to the office and coming home late at night. My big sister became a mother to all of us and cooked. If I asked her when there'd be something to eat, she'd answer, 'Soon, you ass. Soon.'

*

The natives of the Congo know so well that human beings are born to suffer that they pay no heed to suffering. They do not perceive it. They do not know what suffering is. They do not have a word for it. To us, they are cruel, but only to us. For them, killing is taken for granted. If they live to see dusk, to see dawn, it is only because the sylvan gods, or the devils of the jungle, have overlooked them. Have not taken any notice of them for a day. They know no demons who love; such demons simply don't exist. With no emotion, they walk over the corpses of those who fell victim to the higher beings. Neighbours, relations. They are like the animals of their jungle forests. Carry death within, but know nothing about it.—The whole country, the heart of Africa, is jungle forest. Green, moist, eternal. You can work your way forward with a machete for years and you will still be in the jungle forest. There is no way out. There is no memory, no future. The present is unconscious. Trees, more trees, high as the sky. Vines, coiling around them. A predator may be concealed in them. In the grass, a snake. When, gasping with effort, you reach your hut in the evening—that is your good luck. You do not have a word for luck either. You are clueless. On the nights of the full moon, you offer fruits to the powerful; on very sacred days—days only the masked conjurers know about—you offer your father. A child. Oh no—it is you whom the magi drag to the sacrificial site. While you resist, try to beg for your life, you recognize them beneath the masks—your neighbour, your friend, your brother. Strangers now.—It is hot. The water is fresh. The fruit is juicy. Tomorrow you will be dead. Others will walk over your corpse. Dogs will drag the bones off your skeleton. Play with them, heedlessly, until a panther pounces on their necks.

*

Of course, I spoke immediately—Herr Berger was still smiling at the subject of fate agitating me so much—

about Hansi. How different he was! 'Or take my friend, Hansi,' I said. 'He was made of fate!' I was still on my knees. 'The best friend I ever had.' Sweat was running down my brows and cheeks. 'With the two fingers on his right hand, he could whistle better than I could with all five.'

'Where'd he left the other three?' Herr Berger said, shifting onto his free leg.

I knew he was waiting for his *heure de l'apéritif*, the time for his first sip, when he could finally shuffle over to Zur Glocke, the restaurant. There, he would order a Campari or, if it was near the end of the month, a glass of red wine. The *heure* was at six; now it was only about half past four. He'd have to hold out for another hour and a half. Outside, swallows scattered across the sky, shaken by wind gusts. The one cloud had become bigger, and black.

'He blasted them off,' I said, ramming the knife into the lino in such a way that it trembled where it struck. 'His father . . . it was who—'

The telephone rang, out in the corridor. With Frau Schroth, Herr Berger had engaged in veritable races each time it rang; even now, with his rival dead, he ran the few metres. Lifted the receiver and said, 'Sister Anne speaking. What can I do for you?' He spoke in a ridiculously high falsetto, nothing at all like Sister Anne's voice.

He listened carefully. 'One moment!' He then falsettoed, looked at the receiver as if he were praying, put it to his ear again and said, in his normal voice, 'Yes? Herr Berger speaking.'

Why did he do that? He didn't often receive calls. Had two sons, no one other than them. It was one of them who was speaking now as Herr Berger beamed from ear to ear. He began, veritably, to glow. Perhaps it was the son from America, who called once a year at best. 'You don't say,' said Herr Berger. 'Eighteen francs for a portion of meringue!' It must have been the son in Emmental, after all.

I pulled the knife out of the lino. A glaring slit remained. I liked Herr Berger. Compared to many others on the floor, Frau Zmutt or Herr Andermatten, for example, he was likeableness personified. Immediately on his admission to the home, about five years ago, he'd explained to me that it was clear to him that Death crept about in here. Wasn't it only logical, with so many ancients huddled in one place? In his case though, the skeleton had sliced his own finger. Had tried once, half a century ago, with no success. When Herr Berger hears the hiss of the scythe, he jumps aside, faster than lightning, he told me. He demonstrated. We laughed.

'Wait, will you!' he was now shouting into the mouthpiece of the phone. 'Kurt!'

Then he looked at the receiver, as before, except more perplexed. 'Just hangs up!' He replaced the receiver on the cradle. His hands were trembling. 'Kurt. Didn't I just want to tell him—' He went over to the window and opened it. I craned my neck so my face could get some of the new air. True, the air was still glowing hot but at least it didn't smell of polish.

'Hansi lived in the house opposite,' I told Herr Berger's back. 'Up there, at our edge of the forest, were only three houses in total. The day he turned up in our garden, he was four. I was three. Still tied to my mother's apron strings.'

'I just wanted to tell him,' Herr Berger said, turning back to me, 'that in my day a meringue cost one-eighty.'

'Who?'

'Kurt.'

'I'm telling you about Hansi!'

Something in me wanted me to roar. Because of all the chewing gum probably, or because of my father who, at any moment, could arrive up the stairs. He'd hardly be in the door, of course, before he'd be mouthing off about the furniture in his new room, or the horrible wallpaper.

If Herr Berger said anything now—no matter what—I would have roared. But he was looking down, silently, at the garden.

'From that first day, Hansi and I were inseparable. Hand in hand, we went to kindergarten, and Hansi got a hug from the woman. At school, I sat behind him—he had to repeat a year because his first year wasn't a success—and whispered all the answers to him until he was top of the class. *He* set the hedge of the villa next door alight, but that evening the police turned up at *our* door. I got stuck in the sliding gravel of a quarry, screaming for my life as the gravel kept sliding until it buried me up to my neck, he went home. We shared our playtime snacks, he ate his and mine. We rode a tandem, him at the back, me in the front, and, upon arrival, he was brimming with energy whereas I fell into the grass, gasping for breath. He lent me his catapult. 'Over there, can you hit that?' he said, giving me his best stone. I fired it, and it did indeed crash into the glass panes of the villa's winter garden. Was I proud! Right away, they all came running out—the gardener, the butler, even the lady of the house. I had the catapult still in my hand. We did everything together. I loved him like no other. Even our dog, Ero, licked him instead of biting him. He had a great father. Mine could have learnt a thing or two from him.'

'Is your good father also so loud?'

'I'm talking about Hansi's father!' Finally I did roar, so loudly that Herr Berger raised his arms. I gulped and continued much more softly. 'He was the violinist in the Tonhalle Orchestra. Second fiddle. He wanted to show his son, who then was still quite young, the effect of some explosive or another—dynamite or gun powder, or a mixture of the two—and so they were both crouching, little Hansi and his divine papa, entranced, looking at a Nescafé tin and setting up the fuses, crazy!—and, of course, the tin exploded, ripping three fingers off Hansi's right hand and three fingers off his father's left. Madness. Neither of them was the least bit affected. Not at all! As cheerful as ever.'

Herr Berger nodded.

'It was the last time the father ever played in the orchestra, naturally.' I had to laugh. 'He was left with his thumb and his index finger, and as his thumb had to hold the fretboard, he had just one finger to press the strings with. You won't believe it but he still played every day. We could hear him through the window. Pieces he'd arranged himself. Beethoven's 'Spring' sonata, for example. Sounded somehow modern. So desperate, you wanted to cry.'

'Hmm,' said Herr Berger.

'His mother's lifelong dream was to be a singer. But she didn't become one. All day, we could hear her warbling coloratura. And, sometimes, the 'Queen of the Night' aria. Hansi inherited his parents' talents. He could transform the dullest day into an event. He then went to Africa, Hansi. To the Congo, where the blackest of blacks live.'

Herr Berger now put a leg out of the window and looked up at the sky. Clouds were louring. Thunder rumbled. He took his pocket watch out and held it to his ear.

'In my day, we said *negro*,' he mumbled. 'Not *black*.'

I was already in a good mood again, almost. Let him come, my soft-brained father, and let him moan. Maybe he'd get along with Herr Berger, at least. 'When Hansi went to Africa,' I added and sighed—or smiled, 'he took the woman I loved with him. The first and only woman, back then.'

'What was her name?'

'Sophie.'

'Sophie. A beautiful name.'

'I was never to hear from her again. Not from Hansi either.'

*

Sophie and Hansi. Now, of course, it no longer breaks my heart to think of them. After all that has happened. But before!—Even a year ago, when I was telling Herr Berger! How Sophie, who'd been with me that night, then sat in the taxi beside Hansi, a dead expression on her face! Thirty-seven years it's been! Still children we were, almost! And yet, day and night, it would come back to me. She was wearing a white dress—Sophie—and a sandal on her left foot. Her right foot was bare. Between her and Hansi, who was dressed as an Africanist, sat an albino mastiff. It was drooling, had red eyes and was Hansi's favourite. A killer of a brute. It was early morning. Dew on the grass. Birds making a racket and the sun glowing over the trees of the forest. I stood there, with Sophie's other sandal in my hand. Hansi, who had a black, no, almost blacker-than-black eye already, was shouting to the driver to drive off—'What are you waiting for?' I ran, exactly as I was, over to the taxi as it started to move and, when I threw the sandal in through the open window, hit my hand against the metal surround so hard I thought I'd lost all my fingers. Mad pain. Hansi turned to look at me. The dog barked. Sophie just sat there and didn't move. I stood, my hand above my head, without waving. The taxi turned the corner at the kink in the forest up ahead. In the sun, Sophie's face—though it had just been as white as chalk—glowed red.

*

So. I've now gathered all the people who brought me here. With one exception. The person in question was standing next to me when Hansi and Sophie left me for ever. He was wearing a dark-red dressing gown, waving a handkerchief, and said, 'Aren't they splendid, those two?' He burst out laughing, fell silent just as quickly, looked me up and down, and said, 'What do *you* not look like, sir?'

I shrugged. 'I'd been in bed,' I said. 'And fell in the brambles.'

He stared at me for a few more seconds, then turned and went back into the house next door that stood, large and massive, in a park full of tulip poplars and ornamental bushes. Anselm-Bräu, the brewery in Horgen, belonged to him. His name was Anselm Schmirhahn, as had been the case with all first-born Schmirhahns since 1664 when Anselm Schmirhahn the First founded the brewery, in Wädenswil at that point still, and didn't dare call it Schmirhahn-Bräu. The name seemed like a burden to him. So he named his drink after himself, using his first name, a tradition handed down to Anselm the Eleventh, our neighbour. My father, who liked to have a beer, always declined Anselm's products, even when there was nothing else available. They tasted like shit, he said. He drank Salmen, and when Salmen Bräu was gobbled up by Cardinal, he shifted to Pils from Pilsen.

Standing up on the balcony was Anselm's wife. Aline Schmirhahn. She was wearing a nightdress, a white paste smeared over her face. A beauty mask. When the taxi came round the bend, she didn't move an inch. Only now, when her—elated—husband vanished like a dancer into the winter garden, did she stir. Behind the reflective panes of her bedroom window, I could see her pale skull again.

*

She'd fallen in love with Anselm as a young girl when, on the other side of the hedge, he'd ridden past her parents' house, somewhere by Lake Constance. As a teenager still, almost. Many years ago now. She'd thought he was a cavalry officer. He'd greeted her as you would greet a lady, and she'd turned dark red. After the wedding, it turned out that he hadn't been wearing a uniform, but gym shorts and an aviator's jacket, and had also been riding a bike. She was a little disappointed, perhaps also because the first weeks of her marriage had been a charming sequence of short kisses, funny slaps and little ecstasies, but not that continuous inundation, the relentless explosions of all her senses that her imagination had led her to expect. Anselm was in the office a lot.

Now she had migraines, or she told Anselm she had. For once, I'd seen her sitting all afternoon in the winter garden, holding iced cloths to her brow,—that evening Hansi and I crept along the Schmirhahns' hedge— darkness had fallen by this time, and we were two Indians, aged six and seven—and suddenly, close by, we could hear palefaces making soft little noises. Had Hansi not grabbed the seat of my pants, I'd have stumbled over them, like a greenhorn. So, I crawled through the bushes on all fours and, gently separating the stalks of a border of decorative reeds, found myself nose-to-nose with Hansi's father. His white eyes, turned up towards his brain, stared at me, blindly. I could feel his breath. Beneath him lay Frau Schmirhahn—I could've reached out and touched her hair—in a silk dress that had slipped up as far as her navel and shimmered, silver, in the moonlight. Rolling from side to side they were, and once, when their mouths parted, Frau Schmirhahn, her voice quivering with pain, said, 'Hansi!' Hansi's father was also called Hansi.

They'd crept under the lowest branches of an ornamental cherry tree in full blossom. 'Hansi!' Frau Schmirhahn said again, breathless now, as if her life were suddenly at stake, and throwing her head back in such a way that she, too, but the other way around, was looking at us. Her eyes had no irises either. Hansi's father's bottom was shaking the tree's branches so violently, the blossom all snowed down at once. Soon, the two of them—the tree above them, like a bare skeleton now—had vanished in the avalanche of blossom. From far below it came their burbling. Frau Schmirhahn's legs were all that was still sticking out. On one of her ankles, the right, hung white panties.

The house, fifty paces away, was brightly lit. From the open door that led into the salon came the sound of loud laughter. Men's voices and a woman who sang a few coloraturas. Hansi's mother. Laughter, applause. The burbling beneath the cherry blossom ceased, Hansi's father resurfaced and, with a very different voice, said 'Boy, oh boy!' I was lying in front of him, still not camouflaged, but he was looking across at the house. Frau Schmirhahn shrugged him off of her, crept out into the open, climbed into her panties, brushed the blossom from her skirt, put on her shoes that had been lying in the grass several metres apart, and floated off. Air-raid sirens started howling. Like every night—it was the last year of the war—the English bomber squadrons were approaching, on their route north. The sky droned. An anti-aircraft gun was shooting. Frau Schmirhahn vanished into the salon. Whistling to himself, Hansi's father pulled his trousers up and, along a wide arc, also returned to the house. *He*'d forgotten to wipe away the blossom from his tails.

'Your father,' I said to my friend as I got up again, 'is invited to the parties of these Schmirhahns. Mine drinks beer at home and doesn't begin to suspect what other papas do.'

'They do *nothing!*' Hansi said. 'My father, I take it, is allowed to play with Frau Schmirhahn. It's normal, after all.'

We could hear a deafening applause. Then a few piano chords, and the fine sound of a violin. 'My papa.' Hansi wiped a tear away. He smiled. In the distance, the droning of the bombers faded. One after another, the sirens fell silent. The violin sang, as if from another world.

*

The party was a house concert, the very first that Aline Schmirhahn had organized, and all by herself, as Anselm had left everything to do with the household to her. Like us, she'd heard Hansi's father through the window—and persuaded him to make a comeback. He mustn't give up on himself. Hansi and I had burst in during the interval. When Hansi's father returned to the salon, the guests thought he'd dusted himself with blossom intentionally, and rewarded him with friendly applause. Aline Schmirhahn clapped the loudest, and Anselm bent over to her and whispered, 'Charming! Really charming!' Hansi's father first played that wondrous version of the

'Spring' sonata—which also enchanted Hansi and me, out in the garden again—and then his own composition for solo violin, consisting of the sounds of the open strings.

We two Indians were standing in a rose bed, spying through one of the salon windows. Before us, and before Hansi's father who, with wafting hair, was standing on a small podium and nodding to his pianist at important entries, sat twenty or thirty guests on chairs decorated with gold, with champagne flutes in their hands. Men in dinner jackets and women in evening dresses. A lot of jewellery. A lot of uniforms. Right next to the window sat a young man in a much-too-tight dinner jacket, his trousers so short the hairs on his legs were visible. Beside him, two women, with rather daring décolletés, who looked like twins. A gaunt guest, with a monocle on his left eye, was looking gloomily into space. At the centre of the front row, an officer with an extraordinary amount of gold on his epaulettes, between Aline and Anselm, who beamed at each other across him. A butler was going to and fro with a tray of glasses. When he offered one to the man with the monocle, he clicked his heels so loudly that Hansi's father got out of time. The guests applauded enthusiastically.

Afterwards, they all stood around, chatting. Serious faces, maybe because of the music. Aline floated from group to group. Anselm, who initially had spoken to the monocle-wearer, suddenly left him standing, raging perhaps—agitated at any rate—went over to Hansi's father, put an arm around his shoulders, led him out into the garden—Hansi and I ducked into the shadow of the wall of the house—and said again and again how magnificently he'd played. Incredible, this virtuosity, his finger moved faster than human beings can think. 'Let's move on to first names! I'm Anselm.' For a while, they walked in silence, to and fro on the lawn. Disappeared in the darkness, then turned up some-where else completely. Right in front of the rained-empty cherry tree, Anselm stopped, put his hands on Hansi's father's shoulders and said, in a trembling voice, that he occasionally needed some solace. Yes, solace! He found it in professional fulfilment, in music and, above all, in friendship. 'Our most beautiful hopes are about to collapse!' Hansi's father took a step back, towards the tree, but Anselm kept up with him. 'Women are some-thing wonderful. But men's friendship goes deeper.' For a moment, I thought he was kissing him.

'By allowing me to play for your friends, Anselm,' Hansi's father murmured after some silence, 'you have given my life back to me.'

Arm in arm, they returned to the salon, where the atmosphere, meanwhile, had lightened up so much that even him-with-the-monocle smiled when the young man with the too-tight-dinner-jacket said something to him.

Not until almost midnight did the final guests leave. Anselm hugged Aline and, as he opened his top button and took off his bow tie, said 'I've found a friend! Finally! Isn't he wonderful, this Hansi guy?'

Aline nodded.

*

Three days later, she and Hansi's father had a talk, in the same salon, while Anselm was at the brewery. Of course I wasn't spying through the window again, but Hansi's father, red with desire, tried to hug and kiss Aline, I think, and she gently rejected his advances. 'We can't do this to Anselm, and not to your dear Marie either.'—'But wasn't it wonderful?'—Perhaps Aline cried a little as she nodded vigorously. 'As magnificent as never before. You have to go now.' She got up and rang for the butler. 'Adieu!' Hansi's father stood there, rigid. No last kiss as the butler entered the room and led him to the door.

At the next house concert, about six months later, a pianist performed, a not very good one, whom Aline told, that same evening, it had been splendid, more beautiful than ever before and that he should now take himself off. A miserable pianist succeeded that one, on the very first day of the peace, when the church bells had rung for hours. The guests inattentive, irritable. At any rate, when it came to the third pianist, the most miserable of all, Anselm smelt a rat, or maybe something or other got into him. All their friends were there again, almost all of them, for a few of the men were missing, including him-with-the-monocle. They were dead, or in South America, or awaiting their trials in Nuremberg. The pianist played what he could, finally an unrecognizable 'Appassionata'. Anselm—the millionaire!—passed a plate around, 'for the needy artist,' he—the millionaire!—passed a plate around, which led to all the guests, yes, donating a bank bill, but also—immediately after the final bill—rushing to fetch their coats and leaving the house with stony expressions. A scandal. Anselm stood green with fright among the Louis chairs, several of which had been knocked over. He'd wanted to damage the lover, not himself! Aline's eyes were wide open and she was breathing heavily. The pianist was still standing, bowing, at the grand piano, as if expecting applause nonetheless. A deathly hush. Only when the butler put the glass he had in his hand gently down on the tray did Anselm wake up, push Aline aside and grab the pianist by the throat. 'Blackguard!' He was groaning, the lover, as Anselm gripped him tightly, and Aline, sobbing loudly, pulled at her husband's dinner jacket. The butler put the tray down on the sideboard and hit the open palm of his left hand with the clenched fist that was his right. 'Harder, Herr

Schmirhahn!' he cried. Aline, becoming aware of him, chased him out. 'See to the kitchen, Henner!'

They proceeded to drink all the alcohol that was available, still crying, dishing out slaps and pulling each other's hair. At midnight, Aline had confessed—to both her men—of having had the ultimate intimacy with their rivals that neither, in their dreams, could have begun to suspect. 'With Hansi?' Anselm roared. 'On the day he became my friend? We had no secrets! He was living off his disability pension! I paid his rent! And he sleeps with *you*!'

All three were by now so drunk and horny that Aline more or less slipped out of her evening dress unaided, and Anselm and the lover, more than dishevelled themselves, began licking their way about her together. The lover slapped Anselm's behind with both hands as the latter banged his wife, and Anselm urged his friend on when his head was between Aline's thighs. 'You show her, Hansi!' 'Klaus!' the lover burbled. 'My name's Klaus!'

Later still, curled up indiscriminately in one another, they fell asleep on the carpet, and when Aline woke at dawn, she had an unspeakable headache. Everything was booming. Knocked-over wine bottles. Broken glasses. Their clothes were hanging on three chairs, each in a very different place. The two men were lying next to each other, snoring, their privates blue from effort. She showed the lover to the door before he was properly awake. Threw his jacket and trousers out after him. When she returned to the salon, Anselm was sitting in a puddle of red wine and rubbing his eyes. 'I'm going to kill him,' he said. He went into the bathroom and vomitted. Without a word, Aline began to tidy up.

*

Hansi's father died a few months later. Without any effort from Anselm. He fell off Hockenhorn, a harmless climbing challenge, when his fingerless hand reached for a hold in the rock. Time passed, a lot of time, by when his son had grown up, *my* Hansi, and was on his way to Africa. To Kisangani, to be exact. In the deepest of Congo.

Anselm Schmirhahn's grandfather, you see, Anselm the Ninth, hadn't only transferred the brewery from Wädenswil to Horgen, but, swept along by the new colonialism then in full swing—the good old Swiss Franc played a part too—had also wrested a concession from the king of Belgium, Leopold II, that permitted him to run a brewery in his dominion. True, it was not down on the coast as he'd wished—in Kinshasa, and only just renamed Leopoldville—but up-country. Nothing but jungle, and here and there a clearing with a few round huts. Nonetheless, the Société de Brasserie Anselme du

Congo was an immediate success. Per capita consumption in the hot, muggy climate was overwhelming. Beer was exactly what everyone had been waiting for. The customers were, of course, natives—just like the workers who brewed it. Only the directors were white.

Hansi went to the Congo—and so suddenly, above all—because Anselm Schmirhahn had received a telegram. The butler had brought it into the salon on a silver tray. And now Anselm was standing at the tea table, staring at the pale grey form filled in block capitals. He raised his head and said to the picture of one of his ancestors, hanging in a gold frame above the grand piano, 'Hansi! Hansi's son!' He burst out laughing, the same laugh I was to hear the next morning. 'I'm going to kill him. If not the father, then the son.' He sent Henner into the house diagonally across from where they were. Less than five minutes later, Hansi was sitting on one of the chairs decorated in gold, in an elegant suit that made him look like a gigolo. 'You have the makings of a first-class boss!' Anselm said. 'And as far as I know, the financial situation your father bequeathed to you is desperate.' He looked deep into his eyes. 'Moreover, I'm not exactly young any more.' He sighed. 'When I die, the factories in Horgen will need a successor. And that will be you, sir, dear Hansi. That's a promise!'

Hansi drank the whisky, felt it warming his stomach, stood up and said, 'Yes.'

At that moment, Aline came crashing into the salon. Though the sun was practically on its way down again, she was still wearing her nightdress. Wringing her hands, she stopped in front of Anselm and said, 'You'll kill him!'

'The young Herr Hansi?' Anselm smiled. 'This one will survive us all.'

Aline, deadly pale, took Hansi's hands. She'd not done her hair yet and her eyes were wide open. 'Stay here! Don't go!'

'Adieu,' said Hansi.

Aline gave a hiccoughing sob and left the room. Both men stood there, silent, for a while. Then Anselm put his hands on Hansi's shoulders. 'You set off early tomorrow morning.' Hansi nodded. The butler showed him to the door. Clicked his heels before he closed it. When he returned to the salon, Anselm was dancing around the piano, whinnying like a horse and raising his arm to greet his ancestor each time he passed the picture of him. The butler raised his right hand too and saluted again, this time in a more military fashion. Anselm stopped, poured himself a whisky and drank it.

Hansi, on his way home, took out the telegram he'd taken from the tea table and put in his pocket. He flattened it out and read it. Signed by the brewery's bookkeeper, it announced that the director had gone up-country and not returned. They'd found him today, tied to a stake. His tongue had been painted red and he no longer had a penis.

Hansi crumpled up the telegram and threw it into a bush. 'Yes!' he said. 'Yes.'

*

In our country, the birds sing to tell their fellow birds that one of their kind has already laid claim to a feeding ground. In the Congo, the natives sing, night after night.—It is quiet during the day.—The jungle forest sings, rumbles, now in the distance, now nearer. Mysterious drums. Don't go too close, it's not your patch. Creep for your life if you find yourself in the vicinity and a warning song begins. If you see black bodies, shining eyes, it's too late.—The natives chop down circular clearings in the jungle forest, always within double earshot range and, consequently, there is no place in the jungle where you can hear no singing at night. Only when the howling, the humming, the clomping is the same distance away on all sides may you feel a little safe. Sit down on the roots of a tree, lean against its trunk, look up to the leaves high in the sky, behind which you suppose the moon. Press your hands in the wet moss. Listen carefully.—The trees throw back the echo of the singing, just like the mountains do in our country. The echo answers the singers and the singers answer the echo. Again and again, again and again, with more and more daring sounds. Rhythms that are impossible for us to dance to. The natives do dance, as if they

had a thousand feet. Draped with leopard skins. Masks.—
If you're so close that you can no longer escape, mingle with
them. Do as they do. Often they're in another world. Often
they've been drinking beer. But don't sing, don't sing. They
can hear every false note and they'll kill you instantly,
without stopping to sing.

*

'When I saw Sophie for the first time, she was boarding
a tram.' My knees were hurting by now, but I pushed my
knife under the next piece of gum. Herr Berger was
sitting on the windowsill, both legs dangling, one leg in
the room, the other outside. 'At Bellevue, it was. She was
getting on tram No. 2. I stood at the kiosk, as if paralysed,
and knew, it's her or no one.—Are you actually listening
to me?'

'Beg your pardon?'

'Sophie. Tram.'

'Yes.'

'As soon as I came back to my senses, I ran after
the tram, which was heading off over the bridge—
Quaibrücke. It was one of the trams from back then, one
of those moving bowers, with open doors and footboards.
A pantograph like a gigantic paper clip. By the middle of
the bridge, I'd caught up with the rattling thing and
jumped aboard. I couldn't speak, I was so breathless.

Sophie—brown legs in sandals, a bouffant skirt with a petticoat support, blue eyes. She was radiant. I was nineteen, she was even younger. Towards the end of the journey, I had enough breath to gasp my passion to her. She was instantly smitten. We travelled together every day—she lived in Albisrieden, we changed to tram No. 3 at Stauffacher—and it took us longer and longer to walk the few steps from the final stop to her house. We drowned in each other's eyes. Hand in hand, we walked along the lake and kissed each other so hard, we crashed against the avenue trees. For the first few days, she took her dog along, a spaniel; later, she no longer did. Soon we were lying on the railway embankment, embracing each other, even when the trains drove past and bathed us in their whizzing-past light. Me with tossed hair, Sophie having thrown herself on across me, her blouse open. Let them see us, the passengers, our chaste passion. Kissing each other, it didn't ever occur to us that we could sleep with each other. That, no.'

'Aha.'

'Which is to say, we hugged between the sage and the gorse when Hansi wasn't there. He was joining us more and more. Would be waiting where we'd agreed to rendezvous as if a god had whispered to him when and where. I couldn't bring myself to say no to him if he strolled along Seequai with us, or wanted to go to the cinema too. He was my best friend.'

'Hmm.'

'Then, on that particular day—I noticed too late it was our last—we went to the cinema. The Nord-Süd. The first afternoon screening. Sophie was wearing a white dress, almost like a bride, and Hansi a bloody elegant suit. I was the only one dressed like any other day, in cords and a shirt. We sat in the back row, Sophie between us. Her left hand in my right, and her right in Hansi's left. She squeezed my hand at times. And, perhaps at the same time, Hansi's. The one with all five fingers. I was her lover, but she got on well with Hansi too. He was funny! We saw *King Kong*—the monster was heartbreaking when it looked at the little lady so lovingly—and Hansi's comments on the film had the whole cinema laughing.— Had Sophie, at any rate, laughing for sure—till she had tears in her eyes.

'Outside the cinema, she took photos of us, first of me, then of Hansi. He went home. And he'd hardly gone when she started crying and stuttering a story, the only part of which I understood was that her father was terrible. All fathers were terrible, I said, that was just the way it was. She was silent all the way home. She stood in the shadow of the garden bushes and looked at me with her big eyes in a way she'd never done before— absolutely—or in despair—and asked me something in an almost inaudible voice. Of course, I didn't know what she'd said. Her eyes were begging. I don't know why, but

I didn't ask her to repeat her question, instead, I nodded vaguely and stroked her hair to comfort her. Then I wanted to hug her, kiss her, but she tore herself away from me and ran into the house.'

There wasn't a peep from Herr Berger. Dreaming, he was looking up into a sky now completely black. His legs were hanging at peace.

'When I got to Witikon, Hansi was just leaving Anselm Schmirhahn's house. He never went there any other time! In his new suit, he looked more adult than a few hours ago, perhaps because, with great concentration, he was reading what looked like an official document. I asked him for advice. He stood there as if he couldn't see and hear me until, finally, I said, "Well, should I marry her?" At that, he woke up and said, "Yes! Yes!" He crumpled the piece of paper, threw it away and vanished into his garden.

'I then sat alone in my room for a long time, playing the melodies of hit songs on my childhood recorder and looking out the window. Swallows were congregating on the telephone wires. It got dark. Lights—down in the city, above it a bright starry sky. Around midnight, my longing for Sophie and the uneasy feeling caused by her inexplicable look had become so great, I fetched my bike from the shed and rode to Albisrieden. Didn't matter if she was already long asleep. As I tapped my way up the garden path, I crashed into someone coming towards me. Hansi. "What are *you* doing here?" No answer at first. By now, we were out on the street, underneath the light, and Hansi was holding his right eye with both hands. Had I given him a black eye? "What's going on?" I asked. "What the hell's going on?" Hansi stared at me with his good eye. "Sophie's dog's dead. Come on." I'd actually wanted to go and see Sophie. But I got on my bike—Hansi had hidden his in bushes—and, alongside, we cycled the empty streets. By the time we got to Witikon, we were quite cheerful again and fooling around. Yes, sitting at an angle on our saddles, and barely able to separate, we kept telling each other yet another and yet another story.

'Finally, I shoved my bike up the garden path. I'd almost reached the house when Hansi shouted that he was going to Africa early the next morning, by the way. "The Congo or me!" He stood in the doorway, drumming his fists on his chest. "There has to be a winner!" The moon was gigantic and circular. "To Africa?" I shouted back. "How come Africa?" But he was already gone. I put the bike in the shed and went to my room.

'Right behind the door was a suitcase that didn't belong there. I hadn't put the light on and tripped over it into the arms of Sophie who was lying on my bed. She threw her arms around me and kissed me. "What are *you* doing here?" I gasped, coming up for air for a moment.

I saw her naked for the first time. She didn't answer but embraced me again, flooding me with kisses. At first I returned her kisses—also getting undressed as I panted and moaned—but when she threw herself onto me, burying herself into me and biting her mouth into mine, I tore free and rushed out of the room. Out into the open, into the forest. There, I crouched beneath the big oak, its branches trembling, hiding the moon. An owl hooted. Nocturnal animals rustled.

'After some time, I began to feel cold and went back into the house. Sophie was gone and, with her, the suitcase. I called, "Sophie?" once, not all too loud. I didn't want to wake my father, my big and my little sisters. In front of the bed lay one of Sophie's sandals. I lifted it. Then looked across at Hansi's window. His light was on.

'I must have fallen asleep after all, for when I woke with a start, lying crooked in the window, the sun was rising. A taxi was waiting, with its engine running, down on the street. Hansi heaved a steamer trunk into the boot. The mastiff wanted to jump in too. Anselm Schmirhahn was standing in his dressing gown beside them both, doing nothing to help. Sophie came out of the house, walking awkwardly as she had only one sandal and was dragging her suitcase. She had her white dress on. I grabbed the other sandal, jumped out the window and ran down the path. Sharp stones dug into the soles of my feet. When I got to the taxi, the trunk was in the boot and Sophie was beside the mastiff on the back seat. Hansi was at the open car door, shaking Anselm's hand. He didn't look at me, or perhaps he did, suddenly he turned to me, gave me a light slap on the cheek and said, "You did that brilliantly!" Only now did I notice I was naked. With bloody scratches from some blackberry bushes or other in the forest. Hansi sat down beside the mastiff, said something to the driver, and I ran alongside the car as it started off. I managed, but only just, to throw the sandal on Sophie's lap.'

I was now standing before Herr Berger. He'd closed his eyes and seemed to be asleep. Or was he dead? I moved my mouth up to the ear closest to me and blew into it. He blinked.

'Were you ever in love?' I said.

'I *am* in love!' He sounded wide awake and opened one eye, the left eye. 'I'm in love with Sister Anne, I've even asked her if she'd like to marry me. You'll never guess what her answer was.'

'Want to bet?'

'For sure. A bottle of Meursault.'

I told him.

'How do you know that?' Now his eyes were wide open and he was sitting upright. 'Did you spy on us?'

'That's what she always says.'

Herr Berger's eyes got bigger still. He breathed deeply, in and out, and brought the leg that was hanging out of the window back into the room. 'So that's the way it is!' he said, fishing his watch out of his pocket and getting up. '*C'est l'heure.*'

He raised his hat and left to go down the corridor. A buoyant shuffle, if such a thing exists. Outside, lightning flashed across the sky, followed by a clap of thunder.

*

Witness how the tribal chiefs meet in the forbidden jungle forests, and you are lost. On the other hand, it can easily happen. The powerful, in their tribal finery, come from all parts of the jungle forest, taking months to beat their way with knives through the jungle, or travelling down the rivers in dugout canoes. At secret places, they run into one another, run into monsters, monuments, each more magnificent, more gruesome, than the next. They are dressed in lion skins, in elephant skins, are smeared with blood, covered in earth, shine like suns. They wear masks. They are metres tall because they walk on platforms, on stilts made from giraffes' legs, on slaves that have become their legs and who obey them as if they shared the same nervous system. Their dignified greetings last for days as each of them bestows favours on every other, and they all respond to the slightest slight with murder and war. How many shake-hands in the Congo have ended with the deaths of those greeting or being greeted! With the eradication of entire villages! Bow your head to the lords of the jungle—but bow it correctly. Not for too long, otherwise a sword will come down on your neck and you won't see it coming. Bow not for too short a time either—such insubordination will lead to you seeing a flashing knife lunging at you, yes, but you won't be able to get out of its way.—Why do the greats meet? Only they know. When they return, if they return, all is as before—for you. Not for them, but you don't know how. Some have lost their power, without their subjects knowing. For years they continue to rule, all that old terror. Point to him there, her there—and as ever, those struggling and panicking are fed to the crocodiles. Until a child says, 'You old fart!' and the monster falls to the ground. Hands the sceptre over to the child. But speak the word that will deprive him of his power at the wrong time—the powerful one you now suppose to be powerless—and your blood will spray all over the dignitaries, so little time is there to avoid the vengeful blow.—The court assassin knows exactly when to strike. Never however, oddly, has one of them killed the lion-like sovereign, even if he knew the terrible secret—that he'd become toothless—at the last Meeting of the Kings. It is possible that one king devil or the other returns to his tribal clearing—his subjects having sung and danced, night after night—and the souls of all the other ruler demons belong to him, for twelve moons. And he *exploits that, or he doesn't exploit it.—It has been said, I've seen it, that the Unreachables sit in a large circle, with their backs to the clearing, around a blazing fire, through the sparks of which, occasionally, they catch sight of their antipode, a shining black monster made of bloody feathers, his headgear a metre tall, just like theirs. They sit there, they are silent, they sway in response to the drums of the vassals, they concentrate so hard that they attract everything like magnets. Even the jungle forest wanders. People, nearby, huddle helplessly towards the forbidden clearing of the kings. They cast a single bewildered glance at the monster—no! and already, they're the swag of the guards who, with their backs to the royals, focus their attention on the black jungle forest and grab every arm, every foot, that appears out of the thicket. Hold on, hold on tight to every tree trunk, every vine. They can't see you as long as you remain in the black of the jungle forest. Cling with all your might. If one finger strays into the light, it's all over for you. Never ever has a mortal, attracted by the magnetic force of the Eternals, survived looking at the centre of being, that is, apart from, perhaps (as the most secret legends report), one single man who managed to overpower the approaching monster so quickly and take his seat behind his mask that the murderer's aides thought he was the original one.—But you can't rely on that!—The attraction of the—united—chiefs may be so great at times that not only the jungle forest wanders (they begin their meeting in a gigantic clearing and, by the end, are almost crushed by tree trunks), but also whole countries change. Borders that, very recently, were at the top of a line of hills, are suddenly down in the plains. Yes, even continental drift is said to have something to do with the actions of these devil gods. Annually, satellite photos show us tracts of land careering. Trails of dust, swirling water. Goats, people, gazelles running—in the opposite direction—on their native turf which is sliding away. They are slower, though. Backside first, they vanish—still running for their lives on the tongues of the huge monsters—into the wide-open, hungry gobs. Watch out, I know what I'm talking about. You may want to bite too, nitwit. That's what the baboon is thinking too when, desperate, he brings his futile attempt at escape to a halt and, his mouth wide open, confronts the leopard. Releasing that scream that he intends to be a warning, and that the leopard takes as the acceptance of death. The leopard waits for the screaming to cease, and a casual swipe of his paw suffices. Your eye breaks, your neck crunches.—No one knows when these meetings are, never mind where; round about New Year which, however, in each jungle tribe, falls in a different month. You know it when they happen because the singing, the roaring, the drumming is infinitely louder than the everyday variety. The chiefs have heads like mountains, and every skull—each looking so different that, it is said, even the chiefs themselves tremble when they spot one of their kind—every skull, I'm telling you, do you hear, each of these skulls is a musical instrument that produces sounds, the likes of which no one can hear, can bear, can survive. From very far away, yes, of course. Then flee. Flee and don't be deceived by the echo that tries to send you in the wrong direction, into the arms of the curse.— At the end of the weeks-long meetings, when the trees have nudged up close, leaving the remainder of a clearing only because many of them are needed, trunk by trunk, for the fire—when the canoes have been loaded already and the guards staring into the jungle forest begin to tire, when the knives are being used again to clear the path home and no more intruders are expected—the bones of those who came form a pile, off at the side—, when the legs of even the Monstrously Big are sore from constantly concentrating, just as their muscles from never-slackening contraction; then the one who feels surest, the most powerful, says, 'Brothers, how about a beer?' The question is a ritual. The beers are at the ready. But the word must never be spoken too soon. All the rulers drink, swallow, gasp, belch. Lean back. one or other even airs his mask for a moment and wipes the sweat away.—It may be that women, too, are now available for the Great, the Exhausted, but it's always women from white countries, lured to the jungle by charming henchmen, the jungle from which there's no return. Giggling, their skirts already up, aroused, they follow.—The wives of the giants, at this point, turn up anonymously at the markets of other tribes. They wear the most simple of garments, no finery. Their breathtaking beauty alone can expose them and does so occasionally, at which point they are butchered by screaming women. Otherwise, they go here, there. Look for the chief's son. Oh, their eyes. Their lips. Their tongues. Often—always, actually—the young man follows the woman into her tent. To the one who could have been the next lion king, it is as if the heavens have sent her. Naked, slim, expert. She beds him on his back, kisses him on the mouth and chest and lays her head on his stomach—he can see her tight curls from above—and sucks him dry. Sucks and sucks—the king's son wants to melt instantly, with lust—she continues to suck, mercilessly, until his enjoyment tips into pain and he wants to shout, 'Stop a moment!' But it's too late already, he's too weak and she's too strong, so wild in the end that she guzzles all of the chief's son, guzzles him completely, and only his still erect penis remains in her mouth. All the giants' wives do this. The men they imbibe give them the strength they require if they are to be the equal of the Powerful for another year.—With the penis as proof, they return. Some keep the penis in their mouths, like a cigar, most tie it to their belts. Any woman encountered like this must not be killed. In no danger, she marches through the silent army of the mortal enemy. Everyone stares at the chief's son, at what remains of him, in the mouth of the beautiful foe, or dangling beneath her stomach.—Go away, you, if you see a beautiful woman. Hide. She'll make eyes at you. Eyes! Don't trust them, these looks. Or do. It will be magnificent, and your last time.*

*

Herr Berger hadn't been gone for ten minutes when the thunderstorm broke. Lightning struck the elms in the park, and the thunder made the windows rattle. A deluge was descending from the sky. I closed the window and went around all the rooms on my floor to check everything was in order.

When I'd closed Herr Andermatten's windows for him—he was sitting in bed, cursing to himself—and stepped back into the corridor, I heard laughter from Frau Schroth's room. My father's. And indeed, he was standing in the room, stripped to the waist, and one of the cleaners, the prettier one, was towelling him dry. He'd become gaunt, downright scraggy. She was at least as wet as him, and wearing a T-shirt with 'Hard Rock Café Tijuana' printed on it. Her hair was dripping wet. My father was swaying to and fro with the force of her rubbing, and holding on to the handle of a small leather case.

'Welcome, Father!' I said.

He turned around. 'Hello, Son!' The cleaner stopped rubbing his skin and beamed at me.

'Cindy was so kind as to fetch me in the home's VW Bus,' my father said.

The cleaner, who now suddenly had a name—Cindy—took off her T-shirt and dried herself with the long-since wet towel. My father stared at her and so did I, I think. She undid the zip of a pink sports bag, took a shirt from it and put it on. It was one of my father's, a field-grey army shirt from the time of his active service.

'I am from Kramer Junction, California,' she said. 'I studied experimental molecular physics. At MIT, and at the ETH. Graduated with distinction. I'm temping until I find a job.' She spoke with the kind of accent you have to love in order to understand anything that was said.

'Pretty wallpaper,' my father said, the case still in his hand. He stepped closer to it, examined it, a whirl of bright green leaves and maroon flames. 'Really unusual.' Frau Schroth's pictures and souvenir photos had left their mark on the wall. More or less pale rectangles, overlapping in places. I'd taken them down, apart from one I'd overlooked. A large painting. A girl in a white dress hopping across a narrow footbridge, below which a forest stream roared. Above her hovered an angel, in a very similar garment. 'Very nice.' My father stepped closer to the picture. 'I'll keep it up.'

'Don't you want to put your case down?' I said. 'Or are you not staying?'

'*We had a lot of fun, didn't we?*' Cindy said to my father, in English, boxing his ribs playfully.

'*I bet we did*,' he answered, putting the case down in front of the dresser. He spoke with the same accent as her, except inverted. He now rummaged in the pink bag, also fished out a field-grey shirt and put it on. The other shirts he put in the drawer. Then he opened the suitcase and took his puppets out—Hitler and Général Guisan, whose nose was still missing. He and Cindy now looked like two comrades-in-arms, on D-Day or in the réduit.

'I had all the furniture cleared out,' he said. 'One call, and they were there. Did you know that they chop up, there and then, all the things they won't be able to sell? They took an axe to my bench before my very eyes, chopped it to bits, they did.'

'*I cried,*' said Cindy. '*I couldn't help it, I cried.*'

I nodded.

'She said she cried,' my father repeated, in German. 'She's a love.'

'I understand English,' I muttered.

My father joined Cindy at the window which was now open again. He put a hand on her shoulder and she looked up at him. Both smiled. It was still raining but the thunderstorm had moved on. The trees were less restless. The air had become cool and fresh. I stood behind them both. All three of us were taking deep breaths, in and out. Then my father let go of Cindy and tipped the contents of his bag into the dresser—a pair of cords covered in patches, two slippers, a pair of under-pants. The catskin, riddled with holes. His wood-carving knives. A few handkerchiefs. A corkscrew. An ancient issue of *Sie + Er*, with the image of an American bomber plane that had done an emergency landing on the cover. And the revolver.

'Didn't the police confiscate that?' I said.

'They did,' my father answered. 'I re-acquired it when the constable was saying goodbye. The ammunition too.'

'Don't tell me it's loaded?'

'An unloaded weapon. I ask you—' Still shaking his head, my father looked at me, released the safety catch and, without taking aim, shot past Cindy and out of the window. The result was terrible.

'*Hey!*' Cindy said. '*Man!*'

'Papa!' I ran over to him. 'Give me the revolver. Or you'll end up in a psychiatric ward. In a secure unit.'

I put the revolver in my bag. All three of us were now at the window again. Below us, Herr Berger was standing on the grass, eyeballing a pigeon that had dropped at his feet from the sky. Blood, its feathers in shreds. Sister Anne popped her head in the door and said, 'Did someone just fire a gun?'

'Fire a gun?' said Cindy.

'Not in here,'—me.

'A pigeon,' said my father, the only one still looking out of the window. 'It was flying!'

Sister Anne shrugged and disappeared. We remained silent, listening to her energetic, departing footsteps until the sound crossed paths, far from where we were, with Herr Berger's approaching shuffle. Herr Berger no longer sounded buoyant. On the contrary. When he became visible, in the doorway, he was soaking wet and repeatedly blinking as the water was running from his hair into his eyes. His straw hat, which he was holding in one hand, looked like a mop. His other hand was clutching a bottle of wine.

'Pigeons are falling from the sky out there,' he said, in a flat voice. 'Hit by lightning.'

'Fritz?' my father whispered. 'Is that you?'

Herr Berger rubbed his eyes dry. Blinked again. Then went up to my father and, leaning forward, looked at him up close.

'My God,' he said, putting the bottle down on the floor. 'Kuno.'

They stared at each other, shook hands, then remained like that, not moving. Suddenly, they fell into each other's arms and patted each other's backs. Then they let go of each other and my father said, 'This is Fritz. My best man.'

'Your best man?' I said. 'What's that supposed to mean?'

'Kuno was my agent controller,' Herr Berger said, water dripping from his head still.

'Your what?' I looked back and forth, from one to the other.

'We were part of Wiking,' my father said. 'I last saw him fifty years ago.'

Herr Berger held the bottle of wine out to me. 'It's for you. The Meursault, sadly, was sold out. So I got a Kalterersee instead.'

'Wiking?' I said, taking the bottle. 'Never heard of it.'

'Wiking was a line of the Swiss Army's intelligence service in the Second World War,' said my father. 'Our informant was an adjutant of Hitler in the Führer's headquarters. Fritz was the courier.'

'I was a merchant,' said Herr Berger. He beamed at my father and nodded. 'I can't remember if I've mentioned that already.'

'Optical instruments.' I looked at my father again. 'So you were his agent controller. What does that mean?'

'I ran the office responsible for reconnoitring Germany,' he answered. 'I led Wiking.' And to Herr Berger, 'Imagine—us meeting here!' He was glowing too.

'It's a small world!'

The still-dripping Herr Berger hung his straw hat on a cloakroom hook and gave himself a shake. My father took a step towards the bed, to avoid the spray. Cindy, who got hit by some water, shouted, '*Hey, Mister Berger!*'

I dropped onto the plastic stool that, in every room, stood next to the washbasin. I felt as if someone had punched me in the stomach. 'And how come I know none of this?' I asked my father when I got my breath back.

'You were a child,' he said. 'The whole kindergarten would've known the next morning that your father worked for the secret service.'

As Herr Berger was surrounded by a puddle of water, Cindy lifted his arms, took his suit jacket and shirt off, manoeuvred his thin arms into a dry shirt, it too one from my father's field-grey supply, and buttoned it for him. 'You'll catch your death otherwise,' she said when she was done. Now, all three were wearing field-grey shirts.

'After the war, though! When I'd grown up!' I took a step towards my father and, God knows, if he'd not been such an old man, an old dodderer, I might have grabbed him by the collar or the throat.

'I liked being a harmless father,' he said.

'And I,'—I noticed only now, when I wanted to smack my forehead with the palm of my hand, that I was still clutching the bottle of wine—'thought you were a loser! A bore! Useless! A scaredy-cat! A zero! With no fate in life! And the whole time, you just hadn't told me!' I put down the bottle in the washbasin so violently it should have smashed.

My father raised his arms. 'After the war,' he said, 'everyone who worked for the intelligence service during it agreed not to say anything about our activities. And we kept to that. Isn't that right, Fritz?'

Herr Berger nodded.

'You people gave interviews,' I exclaimed, 'You wrote autobiographies. Don't give me that. You appeared on TV.'

'I didn't,' my father said.

'Nor did I'—Herr Berger. And Cindy—maybe because she was wearing the same shirt—'And I certainly didn't.'

All three were now laughing. I gave an icy look to each of them until their laughter froze.

'What your father means,' said Herr Berger, stepping towards me and laying a hand on my shoulder, 'is that we didn't want what we'd done to become public after the war. We had children. And there were a thousand old Nazis wanting to gain revenge.'

He looked up at me—being smaller than me—and nodded yet again.

'*That* was the reason,' I said, nodding too. '*That,* I can understand.'

'That was the reason.' Herr Berger turned to my father. 'Wasn't it, Kuno?'

'No,' my father said.

I'd had enough. 'Food's in ten minutes,' I said and stormed out the door. I may have even slammed it. As I went along the corridor I could hear the two old new friends, in the best of spirits. On the stairs, I ran into Sister Anne who pretty much ignored me.

*

Fortunately, I brought the spare battery for my laptop with me. I've just had to use it as my text was getting paler and paler and, in the end, making no headway at all. The memory was dead.—This is the evening of the third day. I actually wanted to have finished by now. But the end is still a good way off. 76,190 characters have been saved by my laptop. That's the number of times I've hit the keys and I still have ten fingers!—The demons of the jungle forest are observing me. Now that I've embarked on this homage, this conjuring up of ghosts, death is the price to pay if I abandon the project. If I were to go home *now*, a green viper would bite me for sure. I am protected by spirits, but only while they watch. The sufferance of the jungle forest spirits can quickly cease, and woe betide you if you fall out of favour. Run, scream, flee; they'll strangle you when *they* are ready. Then—there you are on your stake, like many others before you. You carry on living for one day, two days, the wood piercing your body. Your screams spouting blood. My programme, incidentally, can only show four digits. That I'm over the limit I know because I know it. It displays only a thousand and such and such a number, each word means a few more, 7,125 it is now already, 7,146 now. Evidently, someone like me—someone who writes *so* much—wasn't envisaged. What, if the machine's memory doesn't have sufficient capacity either?—Up here, there is no printer. No electricity in any case, and I believe the printer won't work from a battery.—I mustn't stop. I mustn't think that hunger is churning me up. That I am stinking. That my back is sore. That I could fall asleep on the spot. I mustn't look across at the beer bottles. The sun is going down. Everything is glowing red. The jungle forest, green otherwise, looks as if it were in flames.

*

When I returned to the room, Herr Berger and my father were still standing. As if there were no chairs. I'd eaten with the Tamils in the kitchen because, for a while at least, I didn't want to see any more old men. The Tamils were young, the creatures of a cheerful god. We didn't eat the institution food—creamed rice and prunes—but spicy rice, and drank tea (the Tamils) and beer (me). The Tamils cracked jokes about Sister Anne and I told them about my father. When I stood up and thanked them for the meal, the assistant cook, Kamal, said it was his last evening. He was being deported the next day. 'My name is actually Saravanpavanathan. Now that we'll never see each other again, sir, I'd like you to know that.' I shook his hand and left.

'Do you know that I—' my father said to Herr Berger.

But Herr Berger interrupted him immediately. 'No! That's the thing! I know nothing! In the intelligence service, you don't share memories! Ask him there!' He pointed at me.

'That's right,' I said, sitting down on the footstool again. Cindy had vanished. She'd gone off to eat, unlike the two old men.

'I want to say this!' My father was red in the face he was so agitated. 'What I'm about to tell you, I've never told anyone!'

'For example?' I said.

'I also had a line to France. That, for example.'

'And?'

'A general in the French general staff. Vichy. Intelligence service man. His name was Lombard and he told me things he didn't report to his own government. I always knew which German troops were stationed where and in what numbers. We met in the Alsace. I crept by night through allotments, through a hole in the barbed wire, across meadows where the ground fog was creeping, and into an inn next to a lock on the Rhône-Rhine Canal. There, we sat in the back room, drinking Edelzwicker. The landlord was in the Resistance.'

'Aha,' I said.

'Oh yes,' Herr Berger sighed.

'Once, when I was about to leave, with a whole stack of materials in my pocket, an SS troop entered the premises. For hours, they roared jokes at one another and sang songs. If only one of them had come through to the back! What's more, the two of us urgently needed to go to the toilet.'

'Oh yes. Been there.'—Herr Berger.

I was drumming my fingers on my knees. Right before me, my father was getting into his flow, more and more.

'Another time, it was the general's birthday. We celebrated and drank a lot. Life then was only tolerable if occasionally you drowned it in Fendant. At dawn we drove to the border, squeezed into the work car, a Chevy,—the whole office, including the women. We crossed over to Germany, still the entire troop, in a boat belonging to the border brigade. There, we took possession of a cannon we'd spotted long since and that stood unguarded on the wooded bank. The women, in their Sunday best, pulled and tugged the most. On the same bark, we sailed back across the Rhine. By then it was broad daylight. Not a shot, nothing. It was a miracle that we weren't singing loudly. On the return journey, we landed in a ditch. The Chevy went over on its side, the howitzer or whatever it was fell out of the boot and rumbled down the embankment. We peed, men and women together, in a long line at the edge of the jungle forest, then walked to the nearest station. The cannon we'd wanted to give to the general, as a present.'

I jumped up and sat down again. Herr Berger opened his mouth, probably because he wanted to say something too. But my father didn't stop to catch his breath, even.

'Any important news,' he said, as if it were part of the same story, 'I passed on to the Allies. That was a violation of the principle of neutrality. If the Federal Council had heard about it, someone from the general staff, I'd have been in trouble. The Allies learnt from *us* that Hitler planned to attack Russia. In the office, too, one single person,'—he drank a gulp of water, mid-sentence—'knew of my contacts—the woman who, always in a different restaurant, met with the wife of the secretary of the British embassy. They had to behave as conspiratorially as if they were abroad. Each carried a newspaper. A copy of the *Neue Zürcher Zeitung*, sometimes the *National-Zeitung*. Inside my colleague's copy we'd stick in the messages. When the women parted after gossiping a bit, the English woman took our paper and vice versa. They always sat near the toilet. If anyone turned up, who looked like someone from the Gestapo or the federal police, they flushed the material into the sewer system.'

Herr Berger closed his mouth again. He'd given up trying to say something. As I had, anyhow. I crossed my legs, folded my arms and looked at my father. There was no stopping him now.

'Once, one of our agents was in danger, in Stuttgart. I'd no one who could warn him and had to travel there myself. It was terribly urgent. I had to catch a train. Sweating with concentration, our expert forged the documents. Passport, leave pass, unlimited residence permit. A whole pile of stuff. All of it more genuine than genuine. Masterpieces. The man who managed to do it all so perfectly stood proudly in front of me, pointing at his watch. Managed just in time. I smiled gratefully at him and signed one piece of ID after another. Then we shook hands, and as we did, it occurred to me that, paper by paper, I'd just signed them with my own name. Kuno Lüscher, and not Horst Wesselheim.'

'That—' Herr Berger said and fell silent.

'Papa!' I said.

'At the beginning of the war, I got a dog from the army. A dobermann. Its name was Ero and it was supposed to protect me. Us. I was so afraid of it, I didn't dare enter my own house if I got home at night and heard it growling behind the door. And so they had to send me the dog trainer too, Herr Harder. Harry Harder. I wasn't afraid of him.'

'Those were—' Herr Berger tried again, again without success.

'Papa!' I said, a second time.

'In the summer of 1942, it was reported to me that Skorzeny was in the area around Singen.' He grabbed the sleeve of Herr Berger's jacket. 'Skorzeny! You know what that means!' Herr Berger nodded, vigorously. 'It was a trifle for him to make his way through the forest from the border—fifty kilometres of the best camouflage—and eliminate me. I slept with a sub-machine gun in my arms. Once, I heard footsteps on the roof. It was him! I took the SMG and climbed onto the balcony railing. Peeped up onto the roof. Nobody. The footsteps had been dormice. I stood there in my nightshirt, like a ghost. Like a target. Not the slightest peep from Ero, and Harry Harder was asleep.'

'Papa!' I said, 'Would you please stop talking!'

'What times they were!'—Herr Berger, spoke at the same time as me.

'God knows, Fritz!'

I jumped up from my stool, rushed over to my father and turned him around to face me. Suddenly, like two hours ago, I had the need to roar. So I roared. I roared, 'Is that true?'

'Yes.'

'What was his name? Skorzeny?'

'Yes,' said my father.

'Did the same Skorzeny,' I roared as loud as before, 'kill my mother?'

My father turned pale. 'No,' he said. 'Not Skorzeny.'

'Then who?'

He shrugged. He'd become an old man again, with a face full of blue veins, fluttering eyelids, trembling lips. A red, crooked nose. Worn-out ears. Like last time, I spoke quietly again. That is, I tried to. But I was probably still speaking as if the two old men were on another distant planet, with their hands covering their ears.

*

'How can you even talk like that?' I said, still loudly enough. 'As if the war had been an adventure! You were fighting for your lives! For that of your children! For everybody's! If Hitler had triumphed, we wouldn't be here today! The old people next door—worthless lives. No Cindy, no Sharon, just Aryan, Helvetian staff. I'd be in a camp, oh what am I saying, I'd have been beaten to death long ago because my father was an enemy of the people. You'd both have been hanged, anyway. And you're both standing there, talking about your glorious deeds.'

My heart was thumping, and sweat pouring down my face. 'The dead!' I said. 'Millions of dead! As many dead as never before in the history of humanity! Heca-tombs!' Could it be that my father no longer remembered? 'Those who were slain on the streets? Those they pushed into canals?' I focused sharply on him and his friend—both of whom had forgotten all this. 'Those in the ghetto? The women, with their children in their arms, pushed down into pits? Pour some lime in, and then the next layer of people? Short-sighted ones, whose glasses were smashed—they at least wouldn't see their end!'

My father reached for the dresser to steady himself. Herr Berger stood there, motionless.

'Those they pushed with poles into holes in the ice!' I went over to my father; he was sweating too. 'Those they herded into shower rooms and then threw the pellets of gas between their legs! Who burnt on the electric fence! Whose brains were removed in operations! Who had to step forward at the morning roll call! Who were shot down, from the terrace, by the camp commander! Who, in the evening, had to play the violin, to German dances, and the next morning they were *selected*!'

I wasn't finished yet. 'And those who starved to death!' I wasn't finished by a long chalk. 'Who froze to death in the ice after weeks with no shoes! Those who clung to the undercarriage of the last plane—in it, those who had sent them to their deaths—and fell when their hands could no longer hold on to the cold metal! Who stepped on mines! Who ran like burning torches! Someone pressed the barrel of a gun against the temples of others and fired. When the low-flying aircraft came, the fun the pilots had as people ran in zigzags. The murderers' grins underneath their steel helmets when the churches started to burn. How the lieutenant stood, between the lavender and the thistles, beside the captured partisans, lit a cigarette and waited until his execution peloton was finally ready. The eyes of the dogs when they sank their teeth in flesh. The white breath of the Gestapo men who hammered doors at dawn. You two could have been gypsies. Sick. Weak. Intelligent. Animals. Have you forgotten them?'

Now, I was finished. Now, I *was*. I sat down on the stool again. My father let go of the dresser.

'No,' he said.

'Not a single man.' Herr Berger was speaking more quietly than him. 'And not a single woman.'

Both fell silent.

'The enthusiasm,' Herr Berger said, finally. And my father, 'We met again so unexpectedly.'

I nodded.

'On the other hand,' my father said, 'we'd no time to be sentimental.'

'It helped if you didn't feel all too much,' Herr Berger added.

I went over to the washbasin and washed my face under the tap. The water flowed over the wine bottle too. I snorted, dried my face and turned to the two old men again. 'My fuses blew,' I said, folding the towel. 'Today's been a hard day. All that chewing gum. And you coming here, Papa.'

*

The storm had stopped, and it was getting darker and darker. In the end, we could see one another only as black silhouettes. I turned the light on. Herr Berger, dazzled, blinked. 'Now it's my turn, eh, Kuno?' he said. My father sat down on the wing chair, crossed his legs and rubbed his hands.

*

He'd been born in the Emmental, Herr Berger. His parents ran an inn that ducked in under a rock face. Its speciality was a meringue the size of a cartwheel. At school, the teacher and all the pupils thought Herr Berger was stupid because he was small. 'In the Emmental, only the ones who at birth look like champion wrestlers are considered clever.' When he was sixteen, he was given a pair of binoculars by a tourist. Or rather, the tourist, who had eaten one of the meringues, left them under the table and when he came back the next day to inquire about them, Herr Berger, who was alone on the premises, knew nothing about them. He was so fascinated by the magnifying glass that he wanted just one thing—to bring the far-off world as close up as possible. To make big everything small. He took the binoculars apart and spent several weeks putting them back together again. But he now knew how they worked. The first time he tested them, he saw—close enough to touch, though she was walking on a distant street—a young woman. Pale, pretty. She boarded a bus and vanished.

He did an apprenticeship in a factory in Langnau that produced magnifying glasses for stamp collectors and protective glasses for bicycle lamps, and soon surpassed his master so much that the owner, an old-school entrepreneur, made him his instructor's successor. And so, at the age of nineteen, he was the technical director. The owner ruled the firm from his villa which, bigger than all the production buildings put together, stood at the centre of the company grounds. As Herr Berger, feeling awkward yet euphoric, sat on one of the huge chairs in the study, smoking the first cigar of his life and pondering the old man's proposals, the door opened and a young woman whizzed in. She was the one, of course, he'd seen through his binoculars. The daughter! She ghosted around the room, not looking for, or wanting, anything in particular and vanished again. 'I immediately accepted every condition in the contract.' The conditions boiled down to him having to work seventy hours a week for his former wage as an apprentice, and assuming all liability for everything. This he then did, and went on to develop a lens, barely the size of a fingernail, that matched the performance of conventional 10 cm optics. OGL or Optische Geräte Langnau (the firm's new name was also Herr Berger's idea) was soon rivalling Zeiss and Voigtländer. Its turnover rose and rose, the owner's profits did too, and one day Herr Berger was again called into the study, was offered his second-ever cigar and a contract that gave him a share of the turnover, and he was permitted to marry the daughter who then walked down the aisle with him—beneath so many veils—he was unsure throughout the ceremony whether it really was his bride, or even a member of the fair sex, who was hidden under all that tulle.

'I remember her,' my father said. 'A really beautiful woman. Did she die?'

'As good as,' Herr Berger replied.

He carried her in his arms, bought her flowers and never smoked in her company. But she just ghosted around the house, silent, exactly as when they'd first met. She sat for whole days in a darkened room, crying, was treated first with cold baths and eventually with electroshocks and, when the war broke out, Herr Berger was the father of two small sons and the unhappiest person on earth.

'To bear all of that *somehow*, I took on sales.' That allowed him to be away from home. He travelled all over Germany. Flags with swastikas were flying everywhere, the trains were full of soldiers, and Herr Berger was constantly having to show his ID. But that didn't bother him much, he was young, everything was an exciting adventure for him, plus, he had a clean conscience, all the more so as he was offering products of interest even to the state. His visa allowed him to enter and leave the country when- and however he wanted. 'I had no political opinions.'

Above all, a special lens, a further development of his very first invention, aroused his clients' curiosity. It was bigger than the original, true, but still relatively small and extremely powerful. He was travelling to

Berlin more and more frequently, to the Ministry of Military Economics and Armaments. Higher and higher ranked officers of the Wehrmacht, and soon also of the SS, sat around him as he explained the advantages of his invention. He did, of course, stop to think from time to time and could guess they wanted to incorporate the lens into one of their weapons. The war was still in its early stages and no one, at any rate not him, thought it would last long or reduce half the world to rubble.

For the weapon manufacturers, Herr Berger turning up was a gift from heaven. Both the cannons of the new tanks and the anti-aircraft guns became significantly more effective with his optical periscope. When Herr Berger realized this, he did all he could to make the gift more expensive and, pretty shamelessly, pushed the price way up. The SS—by now in charge, a general led the negotiations—accepted his conditions after a week of hard negotiating; also, however, because the Swiss Chamber of Trade and Industry supported the conclusion of the contract with a loan of approximately the same amount as the value of the order, as well as, incidentally, a deficit guarantee for OGL. Throughout this period, Herr Berger spent all his free evenings in the company of officers. Pretty soon they were getting on his nerves, primarily because they spoke a form of German that always made him feel they were secretly making fun of him. 'I simply couldn't believe that was how they spoke.

As if their very words were constantly clicking their heels.' Moreover, he didn't get their jokes.

At the end of the second evening, when he'd taken his leave of the officers and almost reached his hotel—he'd risen now, at the expense of the SS, to the heights of the Kempinski—one of his negotiation partners stepped out of a dark gateway and asked whether he might accompany him a little. Yes, of course. He was the technical adviser of the general in charge, a blond member of the master race with a parting as straight as a poker, who only ever commented on specialist questions relating to optics but then did so competently. Prussian nobility. Impeccable manners. He chatted but said nothing special; Herr Berger didn't find him very likeable. From that evening onwards, following their visit to some restaurant, he'd turn up out of some dark side lane, a different one each time. Each time, he became a bit plainer. On the fourth occasion, a light dawned on Herr Berger. The officer may have looked like the Aryan ideal—this too, and not just his technical competence, had indeed moved Hitler to order him to join him at HQ—but he rejected the politics of the National Socialists. He feared terrible things in the future. 'Do you really think so?' Herr Berger said. Yes, he didn't like these hand salutes either, the shouting in the streets, how Hitler screamed on radio. '"I don't know if you're familiar with the Emmental,"—I did actually say to him—"there, someone sounding like Hitler wouldn't have a hope."'

On the last evening, Herr Berger had the contract sewn up and wanted to leave the next morning; the young squire suddenly stopped him in the shadow of an elm and, against all the customs and traditions of his class, held Herr Berger by the sleeve of his jacket and whispered that he, Herr Berger, immediately upon his return to Switzerland, should contact the political authorities. They should warn those in danger of being affected. On 9 April, the Wehrmacht was going to attack Denmark and Norway.

'I looked at him with such eyes! It was 1 April 1940, and for a brief second I considered whether my odd friend was trying to play a trick on me. But he wasn't in the mood for joking. "Do you understand what I'm saying?" he whispered, almost shouting.—"Yes."—"Heil Hitler!" he said and vanished into the night.'

'Force of habit,' my father said. 'The way we say "Grüss Gott."'

'I thought,' Herr Berger continued, 'he was trying to undo what his boldness had led him to do.'

At any rate, Herr Berger travelled back to Switzerland and passed the message to an official of the Political Police who, as he entered the country at the Badischer Bahnhof in Basel, questioned him as a matter of routine.

The official was an awkward man, sucking at a cigar that burnt badly. Unmoved, he noted down the international political sensation in a standard fiche.—On 9 April, the Wehrmacht occupied Denmark and tried to do the same with Norway. On the 14th, at half past six in the morning, someone persistently rang Herr Berger's doorbell. A similarly cigar-smoking, similarly awkward, just considerably smaller, man identified himself as a police officer and asked him to get into a field-grey Chevy. They drove for an hour or two and ended up—not in Zurich, Herr Berger was sure of that; but where then?—in a tiny, almost unfurnished office where a young man was sitting, holding Herr Berger's fiche from when he had entered the country. 'And that was your good father.'

'I guessed as much,' I said, from my footstool.

The fiche had remained lying in the border office for a week, together with many other routine questionings, all marked with the red squiggle at the top of the page that meant 'Nothing Special'. My father had glanced at the fiches nonetheless and read the explosive piece of news. He had almost fallen off his seat. Someone had known what had escaped not just him but, apparently, all the other intelligence services too.

The two of them spoke for more than an hour. By the end of their conversation, Herr Berger was willing to become part of a news line that they tentatively called

'Wiking'. The name was chosen because Herr Berger had described his source—how the person in question had arrived at such secret information, he didn't know—as a Nordic warrior.

'I travelled to Berlin and contacted him,' my father said, turning to me. 'He agreed to meet. Throughout the war, only he, Fritz and I knew who Wiking really was. Even to my boss I didn't name names.'

'Otherwise I'd be dead.' Herr Berger was now standing at the window, looking up into the sky where the stars were shining again. 'He had a dangerous tendency of wanting to show his German counterpart how well informed he was. In March 1943, the young squire and I were arrested. The Gestapo interrogated us.'

'How did you get out?' I asked.

'They had no evidence. Plus, I was assisted from the outside.' Herr Berger left his stars to it and returned to the room. 'Bet you can't guess who that was?'

'Damn right I can. A bottle of Kalterersee.—My father?'

And turning to him, 'You?'

My father shook his head.

'Hand over the bottle!' Herr Berger laughed as if he'd just told a really good joke. I went over to the washbasin and gave him the bottle.

✦

At that moment, Sister Anne entered the room. She'd undone several buttons on her white uniform— she'd finished for the day and thought she was alone in the building—such that we could see her salmon-pink slip. She examined us with a sombre look. Then, however, suddenly radiant and with her hand out to greet him, she went over to my father and said, 'You're Herr Lüscher? Welcome!'

My father jumped up from the wing chair, shook her hand and stammered something I didn't catch. Sister Anne didn't either for she nodded but said nothing. My father, turning red, got completely muddled and fell silent. Herr Berger looked at Sister Anne with so much heart that she, given my father wasn't letting go of her one hand, started to rebutton her uniform with the other. Her feet were in Zoccoli sandals. Her toenails, painted red.

'Aren't we tired then?' she said when she got her hand back and the uniform buttoned again. 'Lights out was half an hour ago.'

She did a right turn, looked over to me—the look was hard and clear and telling me to establish some order here, and make it pronto—and left. We listened to the clatter of her clogs until they disappeared into the silence of the employees' wing. Only now did we move. I walked up and down, hissing more than breathing. Herr Berger held his head back and moved it to and fro. My father did some kind of deep knee-bend and, as he rose again, was the first to manage to speak again. 'I'll ask her tomorrow,' he said, 'whether she would reciprocate my love. I'm keen to know what her answer would be.'

Herr Berger and I exchanged looks.

'I thought you have Cindy,' I said.

'Why should she say a thing like that?' My father looked at me, inquiringly. 'She doesn't begin to know that.'

'That's what she says to everybody,' Herr Berger said. He shook once more the head he'd been holding back. Every single vertebra creaked.

My father tapped his forehead with his forefinger and stepped before the mirror. He massaged his temples, rubbed both hands over his stubble, bared his teeth— yellow plugs—and licked them with his tongue. He leant forward and stared at the end of his nose.

'While we're on the subject,' Herr Berger turned his back to my father. Probably, he could no longer stand his grimacing reflection and preferred to focus on me. 'The Gestapo have a photo of you, sir.'

'Of me?'

'An amateur snapshot, 6 x 9 cm. You're about four years old and standing in front of tomato plants. Your mother is holding your hand. Beside her is a man in a gardener's apron, with a watering can in his hand.'

'Herr Harder! How come the Gestapo has a photo of us?'

'The gentlemen who interrogated me were of the opinion that the man beside your mama was him.' He pointed over his shoulder with his thumb at my father. 'I chose not to correct the error.'

My father removed a hair from his nose with a pair of tweezers. 'I took the photo,' he said, speaking through his nose. 'In the spring of 1942. Someone tore it out of the album on the bookshelf in the living room. No one could get at it, no one. The dog would have eaten him alive.' He took the brush to the three hairs he'd still on his head and asked, still speaking via the mirror, 'Tell me, Fritz. Honestly now. Have I a hope with her?'

Herr Berger went over to the shoe shine kit, removed the tin with the black polish and put it down in front of my father. 'Smear your face with that,' he said. 'And you might.'

*

'In the early summer of 1941,' Herr Berger said, 'I was in Zurich.' We were now all sitting, him on the bed, my father on the wing chair again and me on the footstool. 'I'd been invited by people I didn't know to a garden party. I'd no desire to go. God knows, I'd rather have swum in the lake or just sat, on my own, over a beer in the Bauschänzli beer garden. However, I owed my invitation to a big shot in the Berlin SA who appreciated my impeccable National Socialist views. He was also in Zurich at that very moment and wanted to visit the heart of Swiss National Socialism, as he called it. Moreover, who could know, I might have learnt something interesting.'

Midnight was long past. It was quiet now, no trams any more, hardly a car. Even the screech owl that lived somewhere in the trees at the front of the house was lying in silent wait for its mice. Herr Berger had sacrificed his winnings and poured a full glass of wine for each of us. Only now, after the first sip, did I really regret the fact that he hadn't brought a Meursault. My father, no longer accustomed to drinking, yawned. Occasionally his eyes closed. He knew the story already. Herr Berger was telling it to *me*.

'Not half did I learn something interesting! The address was in Witikon. It was a glowing hot, sunny Sunday, and I was in a garden full of magnolia trees, chatting to ladies in vibrant skirts and hats the size of cartwheels. Many officers of the Swiss Army were there. Even the commander of a border brigade. I was wearing

a borrowed dinner jacket. Not only my acquaintance—
who was as stiff as ever and strutted across the grass with
his monocle on his left eye, explaining how the ultimate
victory would be achieved—but other guests, too, had
travelled from Berlin. They were thronged like gods
visiting the world of mere mortals. They spoke in steely
fashion whereas we country bumpkins growled and
grunted, even if what we were saying also celebrated the
new thinking. I, too, said something about the impurity
of the blood of people from the Emmental. The man of
the house scurried from one group to the other, sweating
with enthusiasm, and the lady of the house floated,
smiling, across the lawn, reviving sluggish conversations
with a funny remark or cheering up momentarily silent
guests with a word of encouragement. Anselm and Aline.
A butler was offering drinks. An anniversary of the firm,
or a Wehrmacht victory, was being celebrated. Perhaps
both. Anselm, at any rate, held a speech in which
Rommel's triumphs in the North African desert and the
success of his beer were inextricably linked.' Herr Berger
turned to my father. 'You—' he said. But my father had
closed his eyes. So he turned to me. 'I nearly fainted
when I looked over into the neighbour's garden. There
was Kuno in his dirty work trousers, tying up beans.
Beside him knelt a woman in an onion patch.'

'That someone might want to kill my father,' I
murmured, 'I can understand. But my mother?'

'She was my closest colleague in the service.' My father wasn't asleep at all. 'She brought the material to the British Embassy. She sat at the teleprinter. More than often, she slept beside it. She could read coded messages as quickly as uncoded ones. Harry Harder should have protected her.' He sat upright and opened his eyes. 'She knew no fear. That is, she died a thousand deaths but kept it to herself. I loved her. She was pretty. We had the children. We carved wooden toys. We climbed mountains. We lay among the anemones. We were happy. It was mad of us to live beside the forest. But it was our house. Our garden. Everything was going well. Everything went so well for so long, I forgot the danger that existed for her. Harry Harder started to think too that he really was a gardener and talked all day about harvesting onions.'

'I warned you,' Herr Berger said. 'Don't tell me I didn't warn you.'

For a moment or two, my father had those eyes I'd seen once before. Grey stones. 'Harry and the dog,' he continued, 'should have spotted the danger.' He leant back again and hid his face in his hands. He mumbled something through his fingers. 'She meant the world to me.'

'And to me even more,' I said.

*

Herr Berger was a guest at the Schmirhahn home twice. Once on a birthday of the Führer, when a pair of twin sisters, in chorus, recited a rhythmically dubious poem, the final lines of which Herr Berger couldn't get out of his head. 'Our Führer's triumphal procession was modelled on Caesar—no question.' The second time was that very house concert at which Hansi's father played his solo programme for the first and last time. 'He was covered in cherry blossom. Odd. Behind him, at a black window, two little boys had their noses up against the glass.'

'They were invisible, actually,' I said. 'Indians on the warpath.'

'My acquaintance from the SA was also there again and shamelessly asked Anselm whether he could remain in Switzerland. Up in his attic or something. Germany was crashing into the abyss. Anselm, instead of answering, suddenly started to chat to the guest nearest to him. That was the artist. He fled into the garden with him.'

I laughed. I could remember exactly. How the two men had walked among the black bushes, faceless silhouettes. I nudged my father who now had his mouth open, snoring as he breathed and, indeed, seemed to be falling asleep. 'Do you realize,' I said, 'that Aline had a relationship with Hansi's father?'

'You're confusing something there,' my father answered, continuing to fall asleep. 'She'd one with Hansi all right. But with the young one, not with the old one.'

'That old biddy? With my Hansi?'

'And how!' My father yawned. 'Once, late into the night, I'd coded the newest information for Wiking into the stock prices that, the next morning, were to be sent with the normal business mail of his firm to Berlin. When I then came home, walking along the outside of the Schmirhahn's garden, I could hear giggling. A man, a woman. I looked over the hedge. They were crawling out from under the tulip tree. Aline was looking for her shoes that were lying far apart in the grass, and Hansi's bottom shone in the moonlight as he pulled up his trousers.'

'The scumbag!'

'Didn't you know? You were his best friend after all. He was laying every woman back then.'

'Really, every?'

My father reached into his jacket pocket. 'Here,' he said, giving me a crumpled piece of paper. 'I helped myself to it when the examining magistrate closed the file.' He yawned again while I searched all my pockets for my glasses. 'Belonged to me after all.' The photo! It had a thousand fine tears. Broken into a dozen jigsaw pieces, my mother was indeed standing between me and Herr Harder whose beard was barely recognizable any more. I was damaged too. Had paled. I was wearing the trousers, made from a red-and-white checked tablecloth, that I'd hated so much. The dog was in the picture too, Ero. Looking very trustworthy.

'Two shots,' my father said after a while.

'Hansi's mother had heard them and called the police. Anselm Schmirhahn was beside himself when, in his guest room, we found a gun with a magnifying scope, two empty cartridge cases and the photo. No! No! That couldn't be! He supported the new—but murder, violence? Never! He hadn't known his guest, he'd been recommended by a business friend, a brewer from Siegen. Indeed, he'd only offered him the guest room because the hotel rooms in town were all full. Every last broom cupboard had already been sold.'

He held out his hand and I gave him the photo back. Put away my glasses again.

'Every woman?' I said. 'Really, every?'

My father nodded.

*

I tell you, over the large towns in the Congo, the rulers in the jungles have no power. Their commands, which in their world mean certain death, do not reach the people in the towns who, deaf to the voices of old ghosts, dig into mountains of waste to find food and drink from pools that are the ablutions of those living higher up. In the towns, the ruling gods don't know their way around. They dare enter them at most once in their lives, and then without their scary masks, without all that rigmarole, and so small, naked, bitten to bits by mosquitoes after marching through the jungle for days and sailing down the river for weeks. The mask they now wear is their inconspicuousness. Their dignitaries are with them, they too without their plumes as they fear being remembered by those in the town. In single file, they walk through the streets, without a map and looking around in panic. They surround their ruler to protect him from adoration, hatred and rage. But there is no adoration in the towns, no rage either, directed at them. No one pays any attention to the jungle forest people. Thousands like them arrive every day. The ruler could starve to death and no one would see him, no one would help him, and many a ruler has *starved on his stroll around town, together with his entourage, as the currencies he'd come equipped with—gold, gemstones, copper wire— weren't those of the town in which the law of the jungle applies, or doesn't. Here, you need your VISA card to pay for your food. Good dollars, a handful of zaires, a few macutas at least or a few sengi, though the latter are worth about as little as the wind.*

The rulers all want to visit a sex shop, a McDonalds, an amusement arcade full of slot machines and, above all, a cinema. They've heard about these so often. No Meeting of the Powerful Spirits where not one of them—once the wrestling for power was over and they, still alive at least, removed their masks—talked about the house in the big town where things could run. I say this because I know it for a fact. And so, the lion-like ruler and his entourage set out in search of the glitziest cinema on the Grand Boulevard. They usually settle, however, for some suburban shack, after getting bogged down in the warren of streets, and then all sit—assuming the woman at the box office accepted their gold and jewellery—beside one another in the first row and stare, more and more agitated, more and more upset, at the screen. They emit little cries and shout warnings at the actors. At the end when—if they've ended up in a western—the Indians turn up behind their white rocks, they jump up off their seats and rampage around the cinema, screaming and howling, hoping to frighten off the attackers using the techniques they know. That they fail, they put down to the fact that they don't have their masks with them, and to the fact that the police come and take them away. Rarely do the rulers visit without ending up in jail. They then stand there, their hands clawing at the bars and being laughed at by their fellow prisoners as they shout that they're kings, viziers, marshals. Completely sapped, totally exhausted, they return to their jungle home. At least no usurper has taken their place on the throne. For that reason too, they'd taken their entire entourage along.— Never again will they leave their jungle forests where they are the lords, the masters, the omnipotent rulers, even if only all too often here a blade is drawn across their throat or a sword is plunged into their guts by their most loyal friend or their dearest son, yes, but that is what they know, it is their world.

To Kinshasa and to Kisangani barge those who have left the jungle forests and can never return. Those who fled from the gluttonous before they could chop their hands off or dipped them in barrels full of scorpions. To begin with, those who fled remember the grimaces of the henchmen, their hut, their wife and children, but soon, rapidly, the images blur. What was, what wasn't? Here a shred, there a scrap. Gone. They have nothing left. No roof over their head, no food, no friend, no forefathers. No ghosts. No ruler.—They only have a TV. That, they do have. Everyone, without exception, has a TV. Take a walk among the huts, not knowing whether they're still standing, whether they've just been built or recently torn down, are inhabited or abandoned, whether they are huts or just coincidental rubble—everywhere, screens are flashing. A blue thunderstorm. Scratchy dialogues from all angles. There is just one TV channel. The people push and shove their way through to the TV. Mesmerized, they look at the lion kings—every programme in the Congo is about them—from whom they

*fled as they murdered Father and Mother. Praying, they
kneel before the screen, not having the courage to turn it off.
Of course, these are jungle kings invented by film-makers,
with monstrous faces fashioned by the make-up artists, in
forests and clearings recreated in studios. It is all done rather
sloppily and carelessly. That said, those praying would still
consider the better fakes as real. As no one, not even a studio
boss, has ever seen a lion god in all his unimaginable
power—a studio boss, for him, would be like some fly shit
on his fingernail—the images that the TV set offers of his
magnificence are so ridiculous, so grotesque, that even the
jungle forest demons themselves, when they creep through
the streets shyly, peering at the screens through portholes and
windows, don't realize this is supposed to be them. Not for
one moment do they consider that these hopping and
skipping goblins are meant to be them. They are confused
by them anyway, for how can it be that human beings are
inside such a small box? And entire forests?*

*Because there is nothing real in the towns—I know for
a fact and am telling you all—the unreal becomes real. All
it takes is for enough people to dream of the same thing, fear
the same thing, speak about the same thing and, all too
soon, it is as real as the rulers in the jungle forest era were.
Torrents of things plucked out of the air sweeping across the
towns that same evening are already a certainty. At the
tables beneath the palm-leaf roofs of the bars, while queuing
for water, clinging to the over-full bus, the people are already*

talking excitedly about the new fact. There isn't one who, barely having heard about it, isn't convinced by today's madness which has replaced yesterday's. Tell someone, 'No, the moon won't roll down the Grand Boulevard this evening' and he'll think you're a madman; the next day, too, when no moon has come. He knows why, you see,—the moon has a family gathering to attend and had to postpone its appearance until next Sunday. Often, a shared madness is harmless, funny actually. For example, if everyone is simultaneously convinced they'll win the lottery. Eight-and-a-half million zaires, even if they didn't buy a ticket, if there is no national lottery and no money that could be paid out. Doesn't matter, have a few beers and forget it. There is always beer involved, let me tell you. Beer is the only real thing in this turmoil of unrealities. Beer always flows with the madness or the madness flows in the beer.

It can very quickly be a matter of life and death. Already, for example, if everyone learns at the same time that, at the other end of the town, tins of tuna are available, Levi's jeans, yes—even free fridges and the free use of cars, and so the entire population, coming from their various outskirts, cross the town to get to the other end, with tin cups on their heads, with carts and sacks, screaming and shoving. Oh, of course—this one or that one is trampled to death in the process.—Beer, beer! No one knows where people always manage to find the few sengi that a tin cup of beer costs. They've always money for beer, even when at home the terminally ill are rolling in their own excrement. Or when suddenly everyone knows   except those affected who will learn it soon enough, too late, and often believe the madness themselves—that the members of the N'Gromi tribe are to blame for the terrible diarrhoea ailments that so many are dying of. That they'll have to be massacred if everyone is to get better again.—The evening before, no one had spoken in these terms. Everyone had still been talking about how UN planes would be dropping video recorders and spare tyres for mofas soon.—Children and women and men are then lying everywhere in puddles of blood, on the pavements, in pineapple baskets, in the suburban trains. A train driver, who is a member of the guilty tribe, is slain while the train's at full speed, and it brings the terminal station crashing down, killing seven hundred waiting passengers.—Beer, now a great amount of beer is needed.— The people celebrate all through the night, celebrate the fact that cholera has been beaten, and some are already buying a mofa and a video film in the knowledge that the tyres and the machine to play the film will soon be falling from the sky.

One madness is the most terrible. For the time being, it befalls the inhabitants of the towns only rarely—though judicious observers have established that this madness, too, is becoming more frequent and, when it does break out, is leading to more and more terrible consequences.—That said, in the towns of the Congo, there are no judicious observers.—No one knows how this comes about but, suddenly, everyone races out of their dwellings and down to the river, up the hills, because they know, know!, that people with lion heads will climb out of their TVs. That they're already outside. Many have already seen one, coming down the Boulevard imperiously, sowing death and destruction. Pale with fright, they describe his mask. The monster's finery is huge! They'll come round the corner any minute, these murderous rulers from the jungle forest, to wreak revenge, terrible revenge, to punish them all for their insubordination in fleeing.—It may be that a real ruler, who happens to be touring the local pornographic cinemas and hears that he's on his way, secretly considers the possibility of showing up, not in his pitiful loincloth, of course, but in full regalia, behind the scary mask and with the lion's mane that have even his own people trembling. I know for a fact and I'm saying it here that—and it wasn't long ago—one indeed wanted to seize the moment and led a triumphal march, passing through the town gates, along the four lanes of the motorway coming from the airport, with all the demons and dignitaries, the court orchestra, the executioner, the flags, the women, the treasury, the crocodiles, and when the inhabitants of the town caught sight of him, they realized immediately that the masked man at the head of this odd procession didn't in the least resemble the murderous rulers on TV. That he was a fake and unreal. They beat him to death. And with him, all his warriors, though they were dancing as they always did and bellowing their roars that had never, to date, been ineffective. Only a few of the women escaped, and all the crocodiles. For a few weeks more, they crawled along the road to the airport until the last of them too had been shot and eaten.

His subjects were awaiting the return of their king. Only rumours reached them of his fate—that everyone was dead—which, as is the way of jungle forest dwellers, they didn't believe. They knew what they saw, and they saw what they knew. They didn't dare elect a new ruler, even when the old one failed to show up for a very long time. What if he were still to come! And so this tribe is the only one in all Congo without a head. Complete and utter anarchy prevails in it. Everyone does what he wants and it's not always the cleverest thing, of course. But no one wants to rule and no one wants to leave for the town. That said, no one dares enter the palace of the king either which, though it once offered space to four hundred courtiers, cowers, tiny, beneath the giant jungle trees. Only the children run through the rooms, sit on the throne and are afraid of the mice and rats.

*

'Now I'll tell you,' Herr Berger said, 'about the visit I paid Hitler. Kuno knows the story already.'

My father was asleep. His head was hanging forward, his chin down. His breath was rattling.

'You knew Hitler?' I said.

'And Eva Braun.'

'I really underestimated you, Herr Berger.'

'You also underestimated your papa,' he said. 'Yourself too. Seems to be a habit of yours. Hitler invited me to his Berghof residence. April 1941. Rommel's tank guns had shot North Africa to bits with the aid of my optical periscope. I was somebody. The young squire came along. He was, after all, Hitler's optical specialist. He was wearing his Sunday uniform. I was in my best suit.'

'I can hardly believe it.'

'So there we were in the Eagle's Nest, high above Berchtesgaden. A room with panorama windows through which we could see mountains glistening in the snow. In the valley below, a white mist. Out on the window ledge, finches fighting for breadcrumbs. In the room— which was more of a hall—carpets, heavy lamps, a three-piece suite. Pictures of the mountains. We stood around, stiffly. Waited. What if it was all a trap?

'After about half an hour, a door opened and Adolf Hitler walked in. He was wearing a loden jacket and a lederhose and stepped up to us in sprightly fashion. Next to him, his dog, one of his Alsatian bitches. Blondi or Bella. Behind the two dogs walked a giant who stood head and shoulders above Hitler. The young squire had snapped to attention and raised his right arm in salute. I, the civilian, had my hands by my sides.

"What a day!" Hitler said, pointing to the shining sun outside. "Rommel's chasing the English as if they were hares. Tobruk is under siege." He rubbed his hands. "In a week's time, the pyramids will be ours."

"Congratulations, Herr Führer," the young squire said. "Permit me to observe that the course of the war is exactly as you predicted."

"My dear Oberleutnant," Hitler said, "there's no need always to be so Prussian. I bet our young friend from Switzerland,"—he turned to me—"doesn't sound as uptight as you. Am I right or am I right?"

'As no answer came to mind, I bowed. The Führer made a sound. A laugh perhaps? "Tea?" he said, going over to the suite of furniture. "Water?" He sat down on the sofa and pointed to the armchairs. We sat down. The dog settled beside its master. The officer hadn't waited for us to answer and brought a bottle of mineral water. He poured us some. Hitler took a glass and emptied it.

"It's remarkable—your optical periscope," he then said to me. "Extremely interesting, young man."

"My company is grateful," I said, "for an opportunity to support the Wehrmacht."

"What did I just say, Oberleutnant?" he exclaimed. "This is how the new man will speak. Pithily. Slowly. In considered fashion. Not like you and your ilk." He looked at me again. "They serve their purpose, the lenses. First-rate equipment, I must say. Exposed to extreme temperatures they are too, fifty degrees above zero by day, minus ten at night. And then there's the sand."

'He poured himself more water—the giant didn't budge—and drank the glass empty once again. "North Africa," he said, leaning forward, "is only a step on my path. A material test. I am busy with bigger plans. I shall attack Russia." I stared at him. But he meant it, was serious. "Von Brauchitsch warns me every day about the Russian winter. A supreme commander who is afraid of the snow before battle even commences! Can you see a Russian winter anywhere?" He pointed out the window. "No Russian winter wherever you look. By September, the whole of Russia will be German. Red Square will be brown.—What a good mood I'm in today!"

'He made that sound again, and this time, it was clear he was laughing. A hoarse bark that made his whole body shake. Even the strands of hair he'd combed across his skull hopped up and down.

"Yes, sir!" the squire said. "Herr Berger and I are in a very good mood too."

"Because, of course," I said, "we've been permitted an audience with you."

"You confederates are always so devilishly formal." Hitler leant forward and slapped my knee with his right hand. "Berger! We're both mountain people! Berchtesgaden isn't Berlin! We're in the Alps here! And both at home!"

'He leant back, spread both arms along the back of the sofa and groaned. The two of us relaxed a little too. Did the squire smile? I, at any rate, exhaled as if a danger had passed, and crossed my legs.

"Hess is due at four," Hitler said after a longish silence. "And at some point, I want to take Blondi into the arena. And that's all for today. The review can't happen until about midnight in any case. The most recent updates will be here by then. If Tobruk has fallen, I'll give the order for Russia to be attacked. By the time you wake up, Russia will be ours. What do you think? Wouldn't that be something?"

"A happy day that would be," the squire said. "One to celebrate." I added, "Your triumphal procession has its model at most in Caesar, back in the day."

'Hitler nodded and put his thumbs in under his braces. He pursed his lips, as if about to whistle.

"Everyone thinks they know me," he said, suddenly upset. "Everyone thinks they know I don't smoke. I don't eat meat. I don't drink. That's what they all think. You do too!"

'I nodded because he was looking at me. Now, he had that famous, piercing look in his eyes, that glare no one could resist. I couldn't either and nodded a second time.

"Do you know," Hitler said, "why no nicotine, no animal fibre, no alcohol contaminates my body? Because that's the way I want it! I can also want the opposite!"

'He turned to the door and called, "Schneider!"

"At your command," said Schneider, snapping to attention beside him.

"Three fruit schnapps—doubles!" Hitler said. "And make it snappy."

"Three whats?" Schneider stuttered. He looked at his Führer with his eyes wide open. "There's no alcohol in the house. At the Führer's express command."

"I want three schnapps—and right away!" Hitler said. His nostrils were flaring.

"Heil Hitler!" Schneider clicked his heels and left.

"Doubles!" Breathing heavily, Hitler waited until the door closed, then bent over his dog, grabbed it by the collar and shook it. The dog—Blondi—yelped.

"I want to discuss optical instruments with you, Berger." Hitler's head popped up—just as suddenly again—above the table. He was speaking very calmly again, as if he'd never been upset. "The development of the science of optics is still in its infancy. I'm just telling you. Very much in its infancy."

'I leant towards him, attentively.

"In here," he hit his forehead with the palm of his hand, "I have hundreds of inventions, all ready to go. Time—time is what I lack." His eyes flared. "I am commissioning you to build a night-vision aiming device. Required amount of light—zero. To be used at a distance of a minimum of a thousand metres from the observed object. No heavier than twenty kilos. The soldier can take it anywhere he goes. Sits in deepest darkness in the field or in the foxhole but can see the enemy as if in broad daylight. One shot and he takes out the foe who thought he was invisible until then. How long will you need?"

"In purely technical terms," I said, "how is that supposed to work?"

"X-rays," said Hitler. "When you buy shoes, they put your feet in a box and can see your toes though it's pitch black inside the shoes. Transfer that system to man-to-man combat."

"My company will do everything imaginable to realize your idea."

'The door opened and Schneider entered, dripping with sweat, and with a tray in his hands on which three glasses and a bottle of fruit schnapps were shaking. He'd raced down into the village in one of the guard troop's armoured vehicles, for sure, and requisitioned every alcoholic beverage in the first tavern they came across. He filled the glasses right up. His hands were trembling.

"Down the hatch!" Hitler said and emptied his glass.

'I wanted to follow his example, though, so early in the afternoon, I didn't feel like alcohol. I didn't get a chance, however, because Hitler jumped up, opened his mouth wide and, staring at me, struggled for breath. He was red, already blue, in the face.

"Schneider!" he gasped. "Schneider!"

'Leutnant Schneider held his hands out—to support him or, if he fell, catch him. But the initial effect of the fruit schnapps was now wearing off; it was, as I discovered when I sipped at my glass too, one of the worst kinds of swill—and so Hitler smiled at his adjutant and said, "Same again! For me, and for these two gentlemen!"

"Down the hatch!" the squire said, tossing it down. I drank mine too and choked almost as much as Hitler. Pure methylated spirit, the schnapps was. The squire was holding his empty glass and standing motionless. Had he emptied the contents into the vase beside him where a few alpine asters were struggling?

'Schneider refilled the glasses.

'By four o'clock, the bottle was empty. Hitler, his legs apart, was sitting on the armchair where the squire had previously been seated. He'd taken his heavy jacket off and undone the buttons of the fly on his leather trousers, such that it was hanging down like a hatch. His hair was all ruffled. His eyes, red. He grabbed me by the tie, pulled my face closer to his and said that Switzerland, kids' stuff, would fall into his lap like a ripe fruit. As the rest of the world would, anyway. "The time is nearing when not another shot will have to be fired for Germany. One nation after another will collapse and fall to me." He let go of me. "I'll put anyone who flees from me up against the wall." He looked at me in a way that made me nod furiously.

'Leutnant Schneider clicked his heels and said, "The Deputy Führer—he's been waiting more than an hour in the winter garden."

"Give him a glass too," Hitler said, handing Schneider the empty bottle. Schneider snapped to attention again and vanished.

"For you, Berger!" Hitler suddenly leant over to his jacket, took a piece of paper from a pocket, scribbled something in pencil and gave it to me.

'It was a business card on which, without any title, his name was printed. On the back of it, he'd written a telephone number—21 1 15, if I remember correctly. I looked at him inquiringly.

"If you get into any difficulty, ring this number," he said. "Strictly confidential. Not even Goebbels knows it. And certainly not Hess. Dial it, and you'll be connected to me as a matter of priority. Whenever. And wherever I am." I put the card away.

'Hitler now fell silent—we, of course, said nothing either—and looked gloomily ahead. Suddenly, radiant again, he said, "I've got it now! I wanted to prove to you that I can do anything I want. And now I want you to go."

'Leutnant Schneider accompanied us. In one of the corridors, Hess walked towards us. He was unsteady on his feet and leant against the walls for support occasionally. As I wasn't walking in a completely straight line either, we had a little difficulty negotiating our way past each other. We managed, thanks to a few Sorry-s and After you-s. Hess smelt of alcohol, but of a different kind. Of Alpenbitter, more. The squire and Schneider had waited for us, both with an expression that swung between understanding and revulsion.'

Herr Berger took the bottle and poured himself the last of the wine. He drank it and, seeing my father asleep, emptied his glass too. I put mine to my lips before he could lay his hands on it.

'Didn't you say you'd met Eva Braun?' I said. 'Eva Braun didn't feature in what you just told me.'

'I had to go to the toilet. Hitler told me where it was. Straight ahead, on the left. I opened the door he'd directed me to. A woman in a pink nightdress was sitting on a bed full of silk, playing Patience with tiny cards. "Sorry," I said. "It's the toilet I'm looking for." She looked at me with eyes that had tears in them. "Straight ahead, on the right." "Thank you," I said and closed the door. That was Eva Braun.'

*

The first light was beginning to shine above the horizon, making the lake gleam. The earliest birds were singing. A gentle wind was blowing. I stepped up to the window and yawned. 'What became of the squire?' I asked.

'He's dead,' said Herr Berger.

'What was his name?'

Maybe it was morning approaching, or my question, that wakened my father. He'd heard it at any rate. He opened his eyes, cleared his throat so noisily, he drowned out the birds, then sat there, awake.

'Good morning, Papa.'

'He didn't want us to give his name.' My father got up and stretched his arms. 'Whether it was Hitler or not,

103

he was a monster or not, Adenauer considered what the squire had done treason. One German doesn't betray another, that was his thinking. Even if it was mass murder, it was your own mass murder. Gehlen Org nagged him so much, he was glad to be permitted to remain silent. Better than always having to face new chicaneries. Better than a trial. No Order of Merit of the Federal Republic of Germany. No thanks. No thanks from Switzerland either.'

'No one said thank you to me either,' said Herr Berger.

'It's all different these days!' I said. 'Everyone would admire you two! You'd be on TV! You'd be celebrated! The *Spiegel* would interview you!'

My father turned the light off and stood there in a pink twilight as the sun rose over the forest above Fluntern. He was looking sceptical.

'That would be something right enough,' Herr Berger said. 'Come on, Kuno, let's out ourselves.'

My father's face became redder, because of the sun, and because his blood had raced to his head. 'Why not?' he said, looking at his friend. 'Except, that will mean we'll have to talk about the squire wanting to escape to Switzerland at the end of the war, and us not letting him in.' He stepped up to Herr Berger so energetically, the latter stepped back in alarm. 'About us not being able to trust anyone in our own service as far as we could spit. About us keeping information from one another. About there even being officers among us who sympathized with the Nazis.' He coughed. 'About many people working with us, not because Fascism horrified them but because they got money for it. About some becoming downright rich in the process.' He kicked the air with his right foot. 'Our laurels are lying among our dirty laundry.'

There he stood, my father, my dear father, shining in the morning sun, in his ancient old army shirt, shapeless trousers and the shoes he'd been wearing for decades to work in the garden. He wheezed.

'*That* was the reason,' I said.

'Yes.'

Herr Berger had joined me at the window. He grabbed me by the shirt. 'He means me,' he whispered. 'He means that I was a businessman. That I sold my goods, that I didn't give them away for free. I *was* a businessman!' He was shouting now. 'That was my disguise! A businessman who earns no money isn't one at all!'

'I don't mean you,' my father said. He sat down again, sighed, lifted his empty glass, looked at it and put it down again.

'But I do!' Herr Berger shouted. 'I mean me! Yes, yes, yes! I *am* a war profiteer! That's what you want to hear, isn't it? That I was a war profiteer?'

'No.'

'That Hitler's tanks triumphed because my optical periscope was so good? That I'm to blame for all the dead?'

'No.'

'But it's true. The German tanks *were* better than the British ones. I *did* get rich. I lived in a villa at Lake Brienz.'

'Doesn't matter,' my father said.

'I could have afforded a retirement suite at Lake Lugano,' Herr Berger roared. 'If I'd not—'

The door had opened, and huddling in the doorway were a dozen men and women in pyjamas, nightshirts, bonnets and cardigans. In the half-light of the corridor, they looked like lunatics who had broken out of a dungeon or some theatre. Clutching at the doorframe was ninety-year-old Herr Andermatten, from the Valais, and within seconds, above, below and beside him, the faces of the others popped up. Not a sound. Just, every so often, a suppressed gasp, a moan, a sigh.

'Everything's all right!' I said with my carer's voice and went to the door. 'Please, ladies. Gentlemen.' I closed the door. I wanted to do so quietly, masterfully, but it slipped out of my hand and banged shut. On the other side of it, Herr Andermatten, who had taken a bump on the nose, was roaring that he'd be going straight to the manager later, to do a hatchet job on me. The others were noisy too. 'Get to bed!' I shouted. 'You have another two hours' sleep still!'

They went back to their beds. The shuffling sounded more and more distant, the clack and clatter of their sticks and Zimmers. When I opened the door, the corridor was empty. Dark, apart from the emergency light. A deep silence and, suddenly, a scream. In the distance, not on my floor, a woman screamed, horrified, unreal almost. At the same time, more or less, I could hear hurried footsteps along the ground-floor corridor— which could only be Sister Anne's Zoccolis. As the distant woman continued to scream, I ran down the stairs, along the corridor on the ground floor and, across the green outside the home, to the service range.

In the kitchen lay Saravanapavanathan, the Tamil— motionless on the stone slabs of the floor. Beside him stood his wife. She had screamed, for sure. She was wearing a blue pinny and a colourful scarf around her shoulders, was wringing her hands and, with rapid movements of her teeth, biting into finger after finger. Sister Anne was kneeling beside Saravanapavanathan, feeling for his pulse, she looked up and put his arm back over his chest. She stood up, rubbed her eyes, took the woman's hands in hers for a few moments. The woman was no longer biting her fingers, instead pressed them against her cheeks, causing her mouth to form a silent scream. Saravanapavanathan was lying on his back. His eyes were looking up at the flu.orescent tubes of the strip lights on the ceiling. In one hand, he was holding the remainder of a black mushroom, the cap of which bore his teeth marks.

Sister Anne closed his eyes. We then lifted him and laid him on the table. His wife, who I think was called Sirah, had removed her scarf and laid it beneath her dead husband. She was shouting—yes, it was she who had screamed before, no doubt about it—that she'd sensed it, that he'd announced what he was going to do, that she'd hoped things would turn out all right nonetheless. That she couldn't get the terrible thought out of her head however—that's why she'd gone looking for him, in the middle of the night, in the kitchen!—that, if the Swiss forced him to return to his own country, he'd eat the mushroom. His country wasn't his country any more, for he would only have to turn up in the village that had been his home, and his cousins and uncles would kill him. He'd betrayed their cause by fleeing. The others, the enemy, would kill him one way or the other anyway, without hesitation, just because he looked the way he did. Everyone had a mushroom like this, every man. In their country, it was the famous healing mushroom— the 'black helper', the literal translation of its name would be—which, if you took a mouth-sized bite, would kill you on the spot. Your life couldn't be saved. Not at all.

Meanwhile, all Saravanapavanathan's countrymen were standing in a circle around the dead man, motionless and quiet, except for a young woman who had put her arm around Sirah's shoulders and, in a low voice, was talking insistently to her. Sister Anne had called the police and the resident physician, and the doctor and a policeman had arrived together, as if they'd arranged it—two similarly friendly, tired men with square faces. They bent over the dead man, then filled out some forms. Each, his own. Just the once, the policeman raised his head and said to the doctor, 'A dead man on the kitchen table—is that in keeping with the sanitary regulations?' The doctor shrugged. The Tamils remained motionless. Only when Saravanapavanathan's wife raced over to her dead husband and lunged at what was left of the mushroom, was there a little commotion. As if they'd all been waiting for that moment, they pulled the woman back. Immediately, she stood there, still again. No one said anything. Eventually, two ambulance men turned up, pushed Saravanapavanathan onto a stretcher and carried him off. He was smiling and clutching the mushroom.

I took a thermos flask, went over to the coffee kettle and filled it. The coffee was actually hot. Someone had turned the machine on. Outside, dew was sparkling on the grass. The sun was higher in the sky. It was already warm. A little further away, the pigeon was lying in its blood. Herr Berger and my father were sitting next to each other on the window seat in the room, waving to me. They seemed to have made their peace. I waved back, brandishing the flask of coffee. The two men up in the window applauded. As I climbed the stairs, I could feel the night in my legs.

*

We had no cups, so we had to drink the coffee from our wine glasses. It was now as bright as day. The coffee did us good. But I was dead tired and yawned piteously.

'We'll go to bed soon,' Herr Berger said.

'But we still don't know who has won the bet. You've still not told me who saved me from the Gestapo.' And to my father, I said: '*You* can go to bed.'

'I've forgotten who it was,' my father said. 'Tell me again.' He poured first himself some more coffee, then

Herr Berger and me some. I sat down on the footstool again.

Herr Berger blew on the coffee and looked at me. 'It was exactly as you imagine. Someone hammering on the door at the crack of dawn. A car with no registration number. Me between two men in grey suits. A silent driver at the front. Hardly another vehicle on the road. Fog. We ended up in a building from the Gründerzeit. In an office where two other men were sitting, in uniform this time, one was heavily built and stuck behind a typewriter, the other slim and wearing an elegant uniform and metal-rimmed glasses.

I was seated in front of a blinding light that dazzled me.

"A spy!" the one with the glasses roared, without a word of greeting. "Confess! Sign here!"—But I was signing nothing. I went icy-cold with fear and thought my only chance was not to know anything. "I sell optical instruments," I said. "How should I know your secrets?"

They had an answer for that. A door opened and the young squire entered with red eyes and a stubbly beard. He'd been arrested the evening before. They watched as we greeted each other, we did so without exchanging signals. The squire was seated on another chair and looked ahead.

"Well?" said the intellectual.

"Of course I know him," I said. "He's my contact person. The *official* contact person."

"As I've been saying all along," the squire said.

"You be quiet!" the heavily built one roared. "Every word you say is taking you closer to the edge of the precipice."

"What are we suspected of?" I said. "If you don't mind me asking."

"Don't tell me you don't know." The intellectual leant back in his seat and drummed on the table with his fingers.

"I don't," I said.

"Espionage for the enemy of our beloved Germany."

"I see," I said.

Again and again, the same questions were asked. Ten times, twenty times. How did I communicate with our service? Which code did I use? Who was my agent controller? How had I made contact with the squire in the first place?

Eventually, the heavily built one reached into a drawer, took out a thin file, flicked to and fro among the few sheets of paper, finally took a photo from an envelope and gave it to me.

"Who's that?"

It was the stolen picture, of course. Of Harry Harder, Nina and you.'

'And the dog,' I said.

'This time, I could conceal my consternation only with the greatest of efforts. I was speechless. When I felt I could speak again without stammering, I gave him back the photo. "No idea!" I said.

"No idea?" He smiled. "No idea?" he roared. "That's your superior! Kuno Lüscher! Beside him is his wife! Nina Lüscher! Who also works for your service! The brat is their son! You see, we know everything!"

"Is it okay if I smoke?" I said. I was a heavy smoker by that point already, worse than now, of course. I didn't smoke Gauloises as I do now, but Parisiennes. Juno, when I was in Germany.'

My father said, 'Their advertising slogan was, *Juno! They're round for a reason, you know.* I've no idea why.'

'Because Turkish cigarettes were flat back then,' said Herr Berger. 'As were the Egyptian equivalent.—Though the two Gestapo men ignored my question, I searched around in my pockets to see if I'd find anything. There was nothing but a little something in the right pocket of my jacket, a card, and I took it out. A business card. I stared at it. "May I make a phone call?" I asked, noticing my voice was trembling.

"No," said the intellectual.

"*One* call,"—my voice was flat, out of the fear that he might stick with that "no"—"and your case is solved. One way or other."

He looked at me. Then he pushed his phone across the table. "God have mercy on you if that's not the case."

I dialled the number. 21 1 15.

It rang once and a voice said, "Yes?"

"Is that you?" I stammered. "This is Berger. Fritz Berger. We . . . "

"Berger!" Hitler—whose voice I recognized only now for sure—exclaimed. "Unforgettable, the hours I spent with you. What an afternoon. Already two years, isn't it?—A mad headache I had afterwards. You too?"

"Not half," I said.

"Hess was drunk when he got here! Blatant contempt for the Führer's orders. The last time I saw him. Offering peace to the English! Not the kind of thing the British do. Must have still been pissed!"

"I understand what you're saying," I said.

We fell silent. I could hear him breathing.

"I," I said but he started speaking again.

"I'm with Speer at the moment. I'm planning a new Berlin. Still a bit crummy, Speer's visions are. I've just been explaining in what kind of dimensions we National Socialists think."

"I've been arrested," I said. "The Gestapo think I'm a spy. Your most loyal adjutant too, only because I know him." I named him. "You know best how unjustified that is."

"My Gestapo?" Hitler rasped. "Is saying you're a spy?"

"Yes."

"No!"

"No, they are."

"Put one of the gentlemen on."

I chose the intellectual. "It's for you!" He looked at me, full of contempt, took the receiver and said, "Obersturmführer Hunn. I'm listening."

He listened carefully. Then shot up, snapped his heels and stood there, as white as chalk, and with the receiver at his ear, turning scarlet. He nodded, nodded, nodded. "Jawohl!" he said, finally. "Heil Hitler!" He listened into the receiver one last time, then put it down and sank into his chair. He was bathed in sweat. The heavily built one was staring at him.

"Why didn't you just tell us right away?" he whispered, the fear of death in his voice.

"Innocence needeth no assistance," I said.

"He demoted me. That's the first time in the history of National Socialism that someone's been demoted over the phone."

The squire and I went over to the door. The two Gestapo men stood behind their desks, their arms raised in salute. The Nazi salute. "Accompany them out!" the intellectual called to the guard patrolling the corridor. "And issue them the document confirming their release!"

Back into the room I nodded, and we headed for the exit. I didn't look at the squire. I had a terrible fear that a whole troop of guards would come running up behind us and arrest us a second time, this time once and for all. Nothing happened, though. We were given our belongings back, and then we were standing outside. The sun was shining. Spring was in the air. Cars drove past. Men in uniform walked past without paying us any attention. I lit a cigarette. We walked slowly along the walls of the Gestapo headquarters. Not saying a word. At the next street corner, we parted without a word of farewell.'

Herr Berger got up. 'You owe me a bottle of Meursault,' he said as he went past.

'Kalterersee,' I said. 'And you've drunk it already. Long since.'

'So I have.' In the doorway, he turned around again. 'Goodnight. Good morning, I mean.' I heard his footsteps in the corridor, then the door of his room opening and closing.

'Time for me too then,' I said. 'Sleep well, Papa.' My father, who looked very awake, waved from the windowsill. I was almost out of the room when I stopped and said, 'I know who tore that photo out of the album.'

'Who?'

'Hansi. I can see him before me. We were flicking through the album together, two little boys, and he took the photo.'

'Hansi?' My father looked surprised. 'I always thought—' He got up, came over to me with his arms wide open and, really, he really did hug me. 'That's good news! And now let's get some sleep, right, Dwarf?'

*

When I stepped out of the main entrance, to walk through the garden to get to my room in the staff building, an ancient Rolls Royce pulled into the car park. Not the kind of automobile that normally visited us. I stopped. An even older man got out of it. He was wearing a black suit, like a minister, and leaning on a stick. He locked the car awkwardly and turned around.

117

'Anselm?' I said. 'Herr Schmirhahn?'

His face lit up. 'My dear boy!' he exclaimed. 'The very person I'm looking for. My project is in luck, I see.'

'If it's an old people's home you're looking for, you can afford better. In Lugano, I know a residence for the elderly with direct access to the lake. First-rate medical care. And you dine à la carte.'

'I'll look for a retirement home when I've retired,' said Anselm Schmirhahn.

He had to be well over eighty. Ninety. He'd a terribly bashed-in face as if he'd been in a fencing fraternity, not only in his youth but at an advanced age too—and lost every bout. His left cheek was hanging at an angle, like a sack, and twitching. His hair, however, was immaculate. A silvery-grey mane.

'I need your help.'

'You? My help?'

'Do you remember Hansi?'

I stared at him. 'What's up with Hansi?'

'For more than thirty years he's been managing the Brasserie Anselme du Congo in Kisangani. A great achievement. I'd never have thought he'd survive even six months. They're tough lads, the negros there. He laughed, an echo of the laugh I'd heard the day Hansi and Sophie left us. 'The money always arrived. Arrived, I say. For about a year, you see, no more has. And Hansi's not responding to any SOS.'

'And?'

'Something has happened.'

'What?'

'That's precisely what I'd like to know. Someone needs to go there and see. Someone who knows him. You!'

'Why me?'

'The climate would kill me.' He took my hands. 'I have no one else. Aline is dead. Henner is soft in the head. No one remembers any more what Hansi even looked like. Just you and me. Please. It won't be to your disadvantage.'

'Ten thousand,' I said.

'Now, now.' He looked at me. 'A little trip to Africa, we're talking about. I'll give you three.'

'Ten thousand. In cash. Or you can get the Red Cross to look for him.' I did a right turn and walked off.

'Okay then!' he called. I stopped. He came hobbling over. 'Bring him back. Dead or alive.'

He counted five thousand into my hand. 'Five now, five when you get back.' He'd prepared everything, flight tickets, a black leather wallet full of dollars, the ordnance map used by the army of Zaire. On a scale of 1:100,000 it was, and it showed the upper reaches of the Congo River, around Kisangani. Even my visa was there. The flight was in three hours—with Swissair to Brussels, then Sabena to Kinshasa. From there, I'd have to see.

I took everything and went to my room. When I took my trousers off to shower, the revolver fell out of one of the pockets. I unloaded it and shoved it back in my trousers. Then I filled my travel bag with essentials— Anselm had called after me that things are always pinched from your hold luggage—and closed the door behind me.

In the corridor, Sister Anne was coming towards me.

'I'm taking a few days off,' I said. 'Urgent family matters.'

'And who'll do the first floor?' she said.

'How about you?'

She shrugged and continued on her way. She was breathtakingly beautiful, from behind too. Especially from behind. Alarming she was, in her Zoccolis. Her blond hair bobbed up and down to the rhythm of her steps. A goddess, someone goddess-like. I watched her as she walked away, turned left at the end of the corridor and vanished.

'I love you!' I called. My voice resounded in the empty corridor. No reply, not even an echo.

As I crossed the car park, I noticed I was singing. Quietly, and out of tune, but singing. I laughed and sang louder. I lifted the lid of the dustbin and threw the revolver in. Waved to Herr Andermatten who, with a dark expression, was stomping towards the main door, no doubt on his way to the manager, to have a real go at me. When the tram came screeching round the corner, I ran, something I'd not done in years.

At the airport in Kinshasa, things were indeed pinched. From my hand luggage, even. A sweaty, badly shaven, very black customs officer waved all the passengers from the Brussels flight through. Except me. I was the only white man. His melancholy eyes looked at me, then he shook his head as he flicked through my passport, page by page.

'*Dans quel but comptez-vous voyager dans la République du Zaïre?*' he asked so quietly, I could barely understand him.

'*Tourisme,*' I answered.

He sighed and emptied the contents of my travel bag on the metal-topped table. He held my boxer shorts and shirts up against the sunlight that fell into the hall via dusty skylights, rummaged in my toilet bag, smelt the soap and appeared to want to read, on the spot, the detective novel I'd fallen asleep over on the plane.

'It's German,' I said, in French, pointing at the page he had open in front of him.

'I can see that,' he answered, in German, putting the book back in the bag. 'Is it any good, this page-turner?'

I raised my hands to indicate I didn't think it was so great. He nodded. 'My favourite authors are Simenon and Montaigne.' As he said that, he felt the seams of my bag and, in the end, put the ordnance map of Zaire, my shaving kit and my sunglasses away in a drawer. '*Importation interdite.*'

He wanted to put my passport away too—but I snatched it, just in time, from his hand. 'I'll pray for you,' he muttered and turned away. I opened my mouth to protest against his haul, then closed it and left through the swing door. The air was so hot, my lungs seemed to go up in flames. A blinding sun that made me miss my sunglasses immediately. About twenty men were all shouting at me. Each had a taxi and wanted to drive me for a lower price than all the others.

The most brutal and, I'd guess, most expensive of them took me to the town centre, to the Intercontinental that, like the whole town, looked as if it had been shot at and plundered in a war. I hadn't found the time to familiarize myself with the most recent history of the state of Zaire and must have overlooked some feuds or other. Ruins everywhere you looked, burnt-out houses, false windows. Boarded-up shops. Gutted mansions, of which only the walls remained. People were walking, all on the way to somewhere. Hardly any cars, apart from my taxi. It did indeed cost as much as in Zurich, albeit in dollars. I paid without blinking. It was Anselm's money. At the Intercontinental, I was given a very acceptable room—one hundred and fifty dollars in advance, I had to pay!—and had the concierge help me book a flight to Kisangani. Unsuccessfully, despite a healthy tip. The phone wasn't working. 'In Zaire,' he said, 'you can buy everything. Passports, proof from the land registry office that you own the Intercontinental, your own death certificate. It's all a question of money. But a phone that works, you can't have. Only the president has one of those.'

And so he sent out several messengers. The only plane of the only airline that flew on that route, however, was definitely lying in the jungle somewhere, with its wings buckled—an emergency landing in a clearing that had almost succeeded, but had demolished a village—and the replacement plane, on loan from the former UTA, was waiting on the airfield of Kinshasa, true, but its two engines had been stolen in the night. No one had seen the culprits, though they must have worked for hours and used a juggernaut to transport their booty.

With the result, in the end, that in the evening of the same day—the room was paid for and remained so—I boarded a ship promising to complete the one thousand five hundred kilometres up the river to Kisangani in just seven days.

It was a barge weighing seventeen and half tons, called *Perle des Afriques*. It was as old as a pearl, for sure, maybe even older. So much rust on all the metal parts, they probably consisted only of rust. Paint had peeled off the ship's rail that, here and there, was missing completely. A deck over which tent tarpaulins with holes in them were hanging and supposed to protect us from the sun. A small wooden hut with glassless windows that rose above the tarpaulin roof, where the helmsman stood at a wheel the height of a man. Behind that, a chimney, a kind of flue, from which black smoke billowed, fumigating the rear of the ship. The captain was a small, wiry man with thick lips, who shouted a lot as we loaded, and later, as we sailed, sat idly in a chair up on the bridge, watching his helmsman as he steered past stumps of trees and reefs.

All in all, about two hundred people climbed aboard, who all wanted to be at the front part of the ship, such that it would have keeled over in the harbour already had the captain not distributed his cargo more evenly by shouting and directing kicks. He spared me only because, also shouting and gesticulating wildly, I had waved a twenty-dollar note at him. He allocated me a corner on the foredeck. Around me, locals were sitting on sacks and cloths; right next to me, an old man who seemed to consist of nothing but wrinkles. He was the one ancient man on board and looked as if he wouldn't survive the next morning.—There was livestock like piglets and chickens too. They lay there, with their feet tied, becoming increasingly listless.

The sun was really low over the horizon when the *Perle des Afriques*, with a hoot,—a horn that would have made ghosts take flight!—sailed out into the glowing red of Stanley Pool. The opposite bank distant in a milky-white mist. I'd expected a sea! A few hundred thousand birds were rocking on the water. I asked the old man why we were still setting out at this time. The Congo River is so dangerous, you can't sail in the dark. Shallows, sandbanks, dead arms. The old man didn't answer. And so I just watched as the skyline of Kinshasa vanished behind us—the sun was getting closer and closer to the horizon—until, after a good hour, we entered the actual river and, indeed, immediately anchored. Around us, countless boats that had all gone into the shallows at some point and hadn't been refloated, forever stranded, each inhabited by at least two dozen people, even if the deck was sloping like a slide.

The sun vanished into the water as if it were plunging into it, the air became blue and, a few moments later, I couldn't even see my hands when I raised them. As a precaution, I felt for my travel bag, to keep a good hold on it, and did so at precisely the right moment for it started to move just as I grabbed it. Someone was pulling hard and immediately surrendered when he felt the resistance. The old man?—In the distance, somewhere on the invisible bank, drums were banging. I got hungry and thirsty and inspected, by touch, the packed lunch the hotel had given me. It was impressively big, but contained—when I opened it—mainly air and, far down, a few tiny sandwiches, a few canned drinks and a lonely something that, when I sniffed at it, appeared to be a radish. I ate it, and also a first sandwich. As I opened a can, the old man—invisible beside me—decided to answer my question and explained that the captain was a member of the wrong tribe—the inferior one, in terms of government rivalries—and preferred to spend the night out in the middle of the river. Onshore, by night, someone like him could easily die. Here on board, traditionally, something like a truce prevailed—so, no murders—as everyone was of course hoping to get somewhere, which, naturally, didn't exclude the possibility of one or other disappearing into the river. On a trip about two years ago, angry rebels had tossed both the captain and his helmsman—both government supporters—in, and, minutes later, the ship had run aground on sharp rocks and sunk without trace. Everyone dead.

'And the white men?' I said, having a drink. A sweet lemonade.

'*Ah ça!*' he grunted and fell silent.

I didn't want to know anything more precise, so went on to ask only if there was a toilet on board. 'At the other end of the boat,' he said. It was so dark, I couldn't even see the contours of the ship. True, there were millions of stars, high in the universe, but there was no moon. I decided to hold on until daybreak. It turned out that all the other passengers had too, and that the toilets consisted of the ship's rail at the stern. On it, men and women were perched alongside, with their skirts up or their trousers at their ankles, and waiting in front of them were others also needing to go. I followed their example, pushed my way forward in the throng and eventually squatted, with my behind in the air and my travel bag on my knees, between a man who was panting from the effort involved and a whingeing child being held by its mother. Before me, and staring, stood the others who were waiting. Below—we'd set sail again— was the churning water. The chimney, at least, was producing clouds of smoke and mercifully concealing us. When I got back to my seat, I was black with soot. I lowered one shirtsleeve down into the water and used the damp cloth to try and look half-decent again.

The river was full of sandbanks, silt and promontories reaching far out into the water. Huge carpets of grass swam past. Often I could hardly see where we were heading. Nothing but jungle forest—ahead, behind and alongside me. Trees, more trees, where there wasn't water there were trees. Giant trees were bending over the floods, as if about to plunge in, something—however—they'd not ever done, from time immemorial. Roots that had the circumference of an oak trunk back home. Other tree monsters were growing straight up into the sky. There was nothing small, rather, there was—as every gap was filled with something or the other that was growing. With vines, with creepers full of red blossoms. With some kind of tropical ivy with huge leaves. Lichen hanging like beards from many branches. Everything was so linked to everything else, each tree was so tangled up in the next, that this sea of trees, this green ocean, seemed to be a whole—impenetrable for anything bigger than a snake or a monkey. And yet there were okapis in it! Elephants! Mysterious paths the natives crept along, invisible to anyone else! Actually, no, now and then, if we sailed close to the bank, I thought I could see black skin flash past, scurrying figures. But I could be wrong. Giant birds whooshed up out of the treetops and flew off over the water. The cries of other animals, death cries followed by a heavy silence. I could hardly take my eyes off the black green. I'd never seen anything so beautiful, anything so terrible. Our ship was crawling upriver so slowly, I was wondering whether we weren't actually floating backwards, back to our port of departure.

Occasionally, a ship came towards us, a barge like ours or a much smaller boat with two or three black men rowing it. Odd tugboats that looked like floating petrol stations, chopped off at the stern; and that pulled up to a dozen rafts, crowded with passengers. On one occasion, a really big, modern-looking ship sailed past imperiously and almost capsized us. After that, the silence was even greater. By day, especially in the late afternoon, the jungle forest was silent. Not a sound and not a movement in it. When the sun went down, though, it got noisy—the animals all woke up and the drums rolled again too, now closer, now in the distance. Occasionally also, drifting to us from far off, came sounds of singing, if this screaming and howling indeed qualified as such.

Here and there were gaps in the jungle forest. Swathes had been cut into it. Clearings where traditional round huts had been built, or modern houses, ugly prefabricated shacks, and factories—cobbled together using corrugated iron—that smoked and stank like they were major corporations. On the jetties—improvised constructions made of wood, really—was clustered the entire population of the settlement. Screams, laughter, shouts—assaulting my ears. Crates were unloaded, the piglets, the chickens. On one occasion, a deep freezer—though the kraal we'd moored at didn't look as if it had electricity. Those aboard the ship tried to sell alcohol, cigarettes or comics to those on land, and those on land were peddling cloth and fruits. The captain loaded new firewood. The helmsman, meanwhile, sat on his boss' seat, motionless, watching the chaos. Beside him, statue-like, as if turned to stone, stood the stoker who, normally, would be stuck in the boiler room in the belly of the ship. He was naked but for a loincloth and a piece of yarn of indeterminable colour around his neck—had it once been white?—that had maybe brought even his great-grandfather good luck.

On the final night, once we'd anchored close to shore, much closer than usual, drumming, singing and howling broke out, of such elemental force that every single passenger—I could see them all in the last of the twilight—either froze or raced to the ship's rail, their faces distorted with fear. Many held on to something, clutched at a heating pipe as if this singing could suck them away. The captain sounded his horn while he still had steam. Later though—by now it was pitch dark—the howling jungle forest people seemed to be much louder. They raged all night long and no one on the ship was able to close an eye, for sure not. I too froze with fear. Once, I heard a splash, as if someone had jumped into the water. A woman screamed. Then all was quiet again. I stared into the darkness but could see nothing. Was that someone swimming towards the singing jungle forest? Had a crocodile just gobbled him up, or was he making it to shore and would soon be on his way towards those enticing sounds?—The next morning, the stoker was missing. We continued without him. The helmsman did the stoking and kept an eye on the pressure gauge, and the captain did the steering.

'*Ah ça!*' the old man said towards evening, shortly before we arrived, as if we were still in the middle of the conversation that, in fact, we'd interrupted on the first evening. 'The white men. I'd keep my eyes open if I were you.'

'Up in Kisangani is the brewery,' I replied. 'There are still white people there.'

'Not that I'm aware of.'

We then went around a promontory and could see the harbour. Flat buildings with large—smashed— windows. Hooting the horn, as we sailed towards the quay in already slanting but still glowing-hot sunlight, the roar of the Stanley Falls—despite all the noise we ourselves were making—got louder and louder. Invisible to us, it had to be behind the tall jungle forests somewhere. There was, at any rate, a rainbow over the trees. Birds were diving into it and vanishing behind the treetops. I went ashore with all the other passengers and the remaining animals. I was clutching my bag so fiercely still, I could barely open the hand in question when I put the bag down on the ground and looked around. Kisangani, which had become a large town after all, seemed to consist of houses made of wood and concrete. Only far in the distance did a lonely tower block rise from among the palm trees, with a huge billboard advertising Shell on the roof.

*

I asked a harbour worker for directions to the brewery. He was the first native to appear not to know French. But when I drank from an imaginary bottle, saying '*Anselme*! *Anselme*!', his face lit up and he pointed to a collection of buildings on a hill directly above us. '*Merci*!'

I didn't have to take a taxi, at least. A little road full of potholes zigzagged up to it and off I set. Like a European, and determined. That said, my legs were like rubber after just a few steps and I was panting as if the angina pectoris, dormant in everyone, were erupting with all its deadly might. Stars before my eyes. But some kind of innate stubbornness—my father, before me, had been like this too—made me shake my head when a car

stopped and the driver offered me a lift. 'Suit yourself,'
he said. '*A tout à l'heure!*' I noticed too late—when the
car drove off, that is—a company car belonging to
Anselme Kisangani, a corrugated-iron Citroen with
a beer-drinking, colonial-style 'Kaffir' at the rear. Oh
well! Somehow, I got to the factory gate. Dripping with
sweat, I entered without being stopped. Wooden sheds,
behind them a bigger, multistorey building and a silo.
Even further back, an ochre-coloured dwelling with a
first-floor balcony. Blue flowers in painted green boxes.
Right at the end of the site was the Citroen, its driver
unloading a basket of fruits and bottles. He waved and
vanished behind the ochre-coloured house. Not a soul
to be seen otherwise. The working day over, everyone
was at home already.

I was about to give up and return to the town when
the door of one of the sheds opened and a woman stepped
out. She was young, about twenty-five, black, and crying.
The tears ran down her face. She was wearing a dark red
dress with a proper décolleté, something evening-dress-
like, and a necklace—looped round and round—made of
colourful fruit husks. On both arms, she had ornamental
rings up to her shoulders. She looked stunning.

'Good evening,' she said in the perfect French that,
clearly, all the inhabitants of Zaire spoke, apart from the
harbour worker. She wiped away her tears.

'Can I help you?'

My legs gave in once and for all and I fell, more out of luck than intention, onto a beer barrel. I was sweating. 'I'm not used to the heat yet,' I panted.

'You never get used to the heat,' she said, immaculate before me. Apart from a delicate black line running down from one of her eyes—mascara washed away with her tears. 'No one does. You should come to my office sometime. It's hell. I just wanted to grab some air. I do the bookkeeping for the brewery.'

She looked like a princess or, even more, like the president's mistress or favourite daughter. Not like a bookkeeper. I told her so. She replied that on a day like today—fifty degrees of heat, no breeze, millions of gnats—it was vital to pay careful attention to your appearance. To exaggerate everything a little. A little too much jewellery, a dress that could seem a teeny bit *overdressed* (she used the English word), a *soupçon* too much mascara. Others, who limited themselves to always the same T-shirt and jeans and paid no attention even to their underwear, would suddenly flip and throw themselves in the Stanley Falls. A woman had jumped recently, she said, bursting into tears once more.

'Sorrow?' I said.

She shook her head and dried her tears a second time. Then even smiled.

'I'm looking for a man,' I said, 'A man and a woman, actually. Two white people.'

'There are no white people here.'

'The man is the manager of the brewery.'

'Oh yeah?' the woman said. 'Coincidentally, the manager of the brewery is my father. And he's as black as everyone else.'

I gulped and tried to get up. 'But what on earth became of the old manager?' I was still seeing stars, but could keep on my feet. 'The white one. His name was Hansi.'

'My father's called Hansi. He's been the manager of Anselme Kisangani since 1957. You'll have to excuse me. Work is calling. Bye.'

She returned to the shed. The way she moved made her as gorgeous as Sister Anne, the first time I'd seen her. Yes, if Anne had been black and had tight curls instead of her blond mane, she'd have looked like this. A queen. The woman wasn't carrying a jug of water on her head, true, but she was walking like she did. As her right foot landed on the bottom step of the little wooden staircase that led up to her office door, I called over, 'And your mother? What's her name?'

'Sophie.' She turned around to me. 'We live over there.'

The door clicked shut. Over there was the ochre-coloured house more reminiscent of Siena or San Gimignano than the Congo. Christ, I thought, my horror becoming greater and greater—the blacks here, in the course of some tribal battle or other, have killed Hansi and Sophie and put two usurpers in their place and given them their names. Now the brewery belonged to them. That, obviously, was why they were transferring no money to Anselm any more. Hansi and Sophie were stuck on stakes in the jungle forest somewhere. And ever since, the new masters had been calmly waiting to see whether someone from Europe would be stupid enough to come here. Into the jungle forest, into the heat, into their world, where there was no law, or only their law. He who killed faster reigned. Manifestly, I was the one stupid enough. Was already in the trap. I was standing on this dusty square between the sheds of the brewery, amid the roar of the Stanley Falls, and suddenly I had the feeling that black eyes were staring at me from all the windows. Eyes of black people, I mean. The beautiful daughter was behind the reflecting glass of her office and pointing to the house. My assassins, I supposed, were waiting there. I waved. I had no desire to have my penis cut off and my tongue removed. My ears and my nose. Nonetheless, I trotted towards the ochre-coloured house. I was attached to the leash of my fate and—whether or not I liked it—it was pulling me forward.

A steep staircase led to the first-floor balcony, where the entrance was. I knocked, at first timidly, then harder and harder. Nothing. The house was like a morgue. I was preparing to knock again when I pressed against the door by chance and, of course, it opened immediately. Hesitantly, getting the scent of the place, I stepped into a dark room with a few chairs. Shoes, boots, a wooden chest. In one corner, an old typewriter. On the wall, on a peg, a dusty safari hat. Apart from that, nothing but a European-looking broom.

'Hello!' I called. 'Anyone home?'

Complete and utter silence. No reply even from the world outside where, any other time, monkeys cried and car horns tooted. Even the waterfall was inaudible. I opened the first of the two doors in the room and looked into a kitchen. Pots, a stove, plates, a sink. A cleaning rag with a wireless phone lying on it. A basket with fruit in it. Knobbly vegetables, some root veg or other. Bottles of beer in a bucket of water. I closed the door and opened the other one.

A bedroom. A broad bed, at any rate, with dark-blue linen was at the centre of the room. A wardrobe, with women's clothes in it. Through a large window, the sun was glowing in my face, on the furniture, the walls. Numerous photos had been pinned to the white plaster. A photo exhibition, truly. I dug out my glasses and the first person I saw was Hansi, little Hansi, crouching in the garden with his father and fiddling about with a Nescafé tin. Both still had all their fingers. Maybe the tin they were contemplating so cheerfully was the fatal one? Next to that photo, one of Hansi's mother, in an opera costume, dressed as the Queen of the Night, I supposed. Hansi's father, at the summit of a mountain. Then Hansi, in the jungle, adult now, but still young. He was wearing the safari hat I'd seen in the lobby and leaning against a tree, the trunk of which filled the entire picture. In another picture, he had a moustache and was hugging the dreadful albino mastiff. Next, Sophie! She was standing, stunningly pretty, in a flowery dress I didn't know, at the rail of a ship that I very much thought I recognized—the *Perle des Afriques*, that is—and staring, seriously, at the water. In another photo, she was sitting, laughing, on a tree stump with a beer bottle in her hand.—Then there were many photos of people I knew nothing about. All black. Most of the pictures were of a woman with thick, tight curls. Petite, not actually beautiful. In one picture, she was wearing Sophie's flowery dress and holding the hand of a little girl. The beautiful bookkeeper as a child, unmistakably so. The latter was in the other pictures too, often with a black mutt, an ugly mongrel, that she was hugging. Near the window I found even a picture of me! Outside the Nord-Süd, making a face. I knew who had taken the photo.

'Good evening!'

Frightened to death, I turned around. A huge shadow that, when I took my glasses off, turned into a woman, a black woman, standing in the open doorway. She was about the same age as me, wearing an apron and glowing in the setting sun. The woman who was in most of the photos! The one wearing Sophie's dress! The book-keeper's mother! Though I couldn't see a weapon in her hands, no machete, no revolver either, my legs again went as weak as before.

'Forgive me!' I croaked. 'The door was open. And I thought—'

The room was burning in the evening light of the tropical sun. The woman, a flaming beauty, hadn't moved from where she was. I thought I could perhaps flee, but she was standing in the doorway, and by the time I could have opened the window behind me to escape via the terrace, the room would surely fill with aiders and abettors to suppress me. Helpless, I raised my arms. On the wall before me, my shadow did the same and appeared to want to hug her shadow.

'I'm here at the behest of Herr Anselm Schmirhahn,' I stammered. 'I'm looking for the manager of the Societé de Brasserie Anselme Kisangani. And was pointed in this direction.'

'He's not here.'

She spoke French, the natives' version. That soft singing, without any consonants, more or less. The sound of her voice aroused me. Where had I heard a voice like that before?

'And you are his wife?'

She nodded.

'Your daughter told me to come here. Into your apartment.'

'Saba. I see.'

She fell silent again. I stood, staring at her. Whatever it took, I wanted out of this room in one piece. Was it best to say nothing either, or was I irritating her more by doing so?

'Actually, I'm looking for the original manager,' I said, 'The white one. His name was Hansi. And he had a wife. Sophie. She left with him though I'd thought she was *mine*.'

'Kuno!' the woman said, moving for the first time.

I got even more of a fright this time—and stepped back so quickly, I hit against the edge of the bed and fell onto the mattress. My glasses slipped from my hands. I sat there and could see her coming closer.

'Your beard,' she said, when she stood in front of me. 'It doesn't suit you.'

'Beard?' I said, reaching for my chin. It was covered in scrubby stubble. 'My shaving kit was confiscated by Customs. Why, madame, are you using my first name?'

She took off her apron, bent down to me and kissed me. So passionately, I toppled back. She was now lying on top of me. Such a delicate person, with small breasts, slender hips, and yet so forceful! Kissing, we rolled from side to side. Something stabbed me in the back, something sharp, that I forgot immediately. She wrapped her arms and legs around me and I didn't resist. On the contrary, I pressed just as strongly—my clothes had fallen off—and blindly into her. She, too, moaned. Doubled the number of kisses she was giving me. Was it a second or an hour before the tidal waves of ecstasy battered over us? They did so, at any rate, and roaring, we romped around on the mattress. The furniture was dancing. The noise we were making could certainly be heard around the whole area of the brewery and deep into the jungle, perhaps.

By the time the woman removed her mouth from mine and I sank beside her, the sun had gone down, the sky was full of stars and only the weak light from a lamp out in the yard was brightening the room. I burst into tears. The woman was lying, with one hand supporting her head, beside me, watching me. Between us lay my glasses, smashed into a thousand pieces.

'I'm not normally like this,' I whispered, once I'd calmed down and wiped away the tears, 'I don't know how that could have happened.'

'I'm Sophie,' she said.

I stared at her. I perhaps wanted to say something in reply, but didn't get to it as the door was opening again; bright halogen lamps lighted the room all the way up to the ceiling, and before us stood a gigantic, ragged monster in lion and monkey skins, with cats' paws and bulls' scrota around his neck, a demon with a terrifying mug and hair like fire. This jungle spirit was uttering hollow sounds and holding a sword the height of a man in his left hand. I could do no other, I let out a loud cry of dismay, was then incapable, however, of any further movement and lay there, frozen, on my back. The demon danced in front of me, howling incantations. The woman beside me sat up.

'That's enough of that nonsense,' she said. 'You're not off into the jungle forest until tomorrow.'

The monster roared once more—it sounded terrible—reached with his free hand for his skull and lifted it off. A face—just as black, but much smaller and not *so* hideous—became visible, with its round, shining eyes and white teeth. The mask now dangling in the right hand of this strange demon continued to stare at me just as vindictively.

'A visitor?' the man said.

'As you can see.'

'What do you mean see? They can hear you as far away as the source of the Nile.'

'I asked him a question thirty-seven years ago.' The woman gave me a friendly slap on the hands which I'd joined, as if to pray, and placed over my privates. 'Today, he gave me an answer.' She sat there, with her legs apart, cheerful, showing no shame vis-à-vis the intruder. 'And it was the right one.'

'Hello, Kuno,' the monster said, throwing me the mask in such a way, I had to catch it. It was now bang in front of my eyes, and gigantic. 'Don't you recognize your friend Hansi any more?'

The spell that had paralysed me fell from me. I threw the mask on the ground, jumped up from the bed and stood right in front of this grinning chap in his carnival costume. I understood. This, of course, was a trap too! Part of the conspiracy. This person standing before me, whose skin was even blacker than his mask— and it was made of ebony—had Sophie on his conscience, my Sophie, and no doubt poor Hansi too. Now it was my turn. It was already happening—he and his wife were going to disembowel me. First, she treated herself to some love frolics, now, he would slaughter me. Jealousy would no doubt make him even crueller. He'd heard us, all our cries! Maybe she helped him slaughter people, then screamed even more orgiastically, more wildly! The sword, at any rate, was at the ready. They'd probably eat me afterwards. Yes, clearly they'd expected me and bought the vegetables and fruit I'd seen in the kitchen in plenty of time at the market. As a side dish. I stared at this fake Hansi so furiously, I no longer felt afraid. Here I was, their proud victim! What cheek, calling himself Hansi, to boot!

'Hansi was white!' I said. 'And Sophie, even whiter! What have you done with them both? Dragged them into the jungle forest and skewered them on stakes?'

'No,' the man said.

I was in full flow now and grabbed the monster in disguise by his hides, by a dangling lion's claw. 'Killed them, you have! You've raped Sophie, and poor Hansi—'

'What?' the man said as I'd paused. 'What did I do?' He was standing so close, I could smell his breath. Beer?

'You know fine well what the white men think,' the woman said, now also standing and putting her apron back on. 'You cut Hansi's dick off.'

'Are you telling me you didn't?' I gasped.

'No,' she said.

She left the room. The man, the monster, turned on his heel and followed her. I gathered my clothes that were scattered on the floor and got dressed. The glasses, now in pitiful bits, I threw in a wastepaper basket. I could now no longer read, unless it was in bold print. From outside, I could hear dishes rattling. When I stepped into the lobby, the woman, the man and Saba, their beautiful daughter, were sitting at a table laden with food. Hell knows where they'd suddenly got all that from. No halogen light this time. Four fat candles were burning in wooden stands, hand-carved and colourfully painted. The man had taken off his demon's costume— hanging like a dead animal over the back of a chair, it was—and sat there in a white string vest and blue football shorts. The woman was still wearing the apron which, now I could see it from behind, left her back and behind visible and was tied in a big bow. Saba was no longer tear-stained and looked, still, as if she'd be leaving any minute for a soirée. She gave me a friendly smile. As I sat down, a man came out of the kitchen with a steaming bowl, a black cook with a sparkling white hat. He beamed at me like an old friend and I recognized the driver of the Citroen. 'Told you we'd meet again!' he said and laughed. In Zaire, people laugh a lot, especially when they're about to kill someone.

Though my death couldn't be far off now, I was hungry. The tiny sandwiches from the Intercontinental hadn't been enough to fill me. I piled my plate high, ate with a voracious appetite. Exotic vegetables that tasted wonderful. Those knobbly vegetables, now soft-boiled and sprinkled with a red spice. The meat, steaming in the bowl, I declined, however. I didn't feel like meat.

'This is the special bock beer we brew for Easter,' the man said, taking a bottle out from under the table, opening its clamp top and pouring me some. 'Only for dear, special guests.'

He raised his glass to me. His wife and daughter had a sip too. I lifted my glass and tried a gulp. An unusual flavour. Odd, but good. Plus, I now knew what the monster stank of, when you got too close to him. Anselme Bock. *Bière Spéciale*. Through the open kitchen door I could see that the cook at his table, too, was lifting an Easter bock to his lips. He raised his glass to me. I nodded. Above me, on the ceiling, a fan was turning. The candles flickered, submerging us in the kind of light you get in old photos. It was quiet, apart from the rattling of forks and knives, a few very distant drums and the roar of the Falls.

'You can't be Hansi, monsieur,' I said, calmly this time. 'And you're not Sophie, madame. It's not possible.'

'Look at this!' He shoved his right hand across the table. He had only two fingers! 'Don't you remember— my papa?' He played an imaginary violin with his maimed hand, whistling the 'Spring' sonata as he did. Hansi senior's version.

'On the last evening, you caught Hansi in my garden,' the woman said, sounding as if she were expanding on her husband's arguments. 'When I'd found the dog dead. Do you know what had happened before that?'

I said nothing, but looked at her wide-eyed.

'Hansi had climbed in through my window and asked me to be his wife. I'd said no.'

'She wanted you,' said the man claiming to be Hansi. 'I wouldn't let go, also wanted to kiss her, and she gave me a black eye. She went over to you and threw herself into your arms. But then you messed everything up again.'

'I wanted Kuno,' the fake Sophie said. 'I got Hansi. And now I'm glad I did.'

Saba, the beautiful daughter, looked back and forth, from one to the other. 'You've never told me that before,' she murmured. 'That Mama wanted someone else.'

'Every woman wants someone else at some point or other.' Leaning across the table, the strange Sophie put one hand on top of her daughter's. 'Think about it.'

Saba jumped up. Tears were pouring from her eyes. She stood there, trembling, then snarled, 'Deal with your own shit!' She swept over to the door and slammed it behind her. I could hear her clattering her way down the wooden stairs outside and running off across the yard.

'Was that necessary?' the man grumbled.

'No,' she said. 'I'm sorry.'

I had listened to the to and fro, this more-than-incredible story. The two black people in front of me, with their magic traditions and their voodoo, may well have concocted the story in their own minds such that they now felt as if they hadn't murdered but had been murdered. Thought they were their victims. Such that the woman could wear Sophie's clothes and rape me in her name. The man, this monster, had gone as far as to amputate the same three fingers as Hansi.

'You got all this information from Hansi and Sophie!' I said, as coolly as a state prosecutor. 'In Switzerland, we don't know what torture is. Put a Swiss man in a barrel of poisonous snakes and he'll confess everything.'

They stared at me. Silently. Exchanged looks. Their mouths were wide open. The cook, too, as he collected the plates, was gawping. Next thing, the man—a black man in the heart of Africa!—was speaking Swiss German. The dialect of Zurich. *Züritüüütsch*! As if he was from Witikon, one hundred per cent. He knew all of my friend Hansi's expressions. Could even speak like Anselm, in those guild-member cadences that let everyone know he wasn't living off the interest but the interest on the interest on his capital. This strange Hansi had really got going and would have blustered on for a longer time had his wife—black, with thick black curls and thick lips!—not started singing a military march, the 'Sechseläuten-Marsch', also from Zurich.

I was trembling. Dread, I was filled with a veritable dread. Did sorcerers, charms, exist that could give these two murderers such precise knowledge? I shook my head, no, my head was shaking itself. 'No!' The word screamed out of me. 'No!'

'We don't know why we turned black,' said the one claiming to be Sophie. 'We just suddenly were. At some point in the sixties. It's not just superficial, at any rate. Not some change in pigment, caused by, for example, the sun. Our daughter was born black.'

The door opened as if a ghost had opened it. No one came in. You could just hear the roaring of the water more clearly, and the distant drumming that was now accompanied by howling and screeching. When I looked down, though, I saw a dog. A mongrel, not much bigger than a dachshund, with the head of a mastiff. It was black.

'See?' the phoney Hansi said. 'Even the dog!'

'You're not trying to tell me'—the dog was sniffing at me and I patted its hideous head—'that that's your albino mastiff from back then?'

'Its great-grandchild,' said Hansi. 'Pascha'—that was the name of the brute whose descendant this monstrosity between my legs was supposed to be—'turned black even before us.'

'No,' I muttered again. 'No!' The word maybe screamed out of me one more time. The room was swirling around me, or I was turning in it. I held the edge of the table to steady myself and closed my eyes.

'To begin with, we got into rather a panic,' I heard the woman saying from very far away. 'Then we got used to our new appearance. And in the end, we were truly happy about it.'

I opened my eyes. The tables, chairs, the woman beside me too, all stayed more or less firmly in their place. She got up and closed the door. Opening doors, the dog could do. Closing them wasn't something it aspired to. I was gasping and sweating. The man raised his glass to me. We drank from our glasses. A big moth burned in the flames of the candles. We remained silent, listening to the sounds of the house, which were mainly the deep long breaths of the cook. He'd put his head down on the kitchen table and was sleeping. 'Let's get some sleep too,' said Sophie—who couldn't be Sophie.

'Saba has a boyfriend,' said her husband. 'A few days ago, his wife threw herself into the Falls. She could no longer bear sharing her husband. He's now knocking at

Saba's door, day and night. But she won't open it to him.
She hadn't known that he still had a wife.'

He blew out the candles. It turned out that he and
his wife had no spare bed, so the three of us were soon
lying in the bed I already knew. The woman in the
middle. She turned off the light and reached for my hand.
I returned the pressure. I was sure her other hand was
holding her husband's. He began to snore immediately
nonetheless. She needed a bit longer to fall asleep. But
then her fingers freed themselves from mine and she was
breathing deeply and regularly. I looked up at the ceiling,
at the shadows of insects dancing around the light out
in the yard. Should I flee now?

When the morning sun shone into the room, I fell
into a dreamless sleep.

*

The room was as bright as day when I woke. I was alone.
Below the window, workers were rolling barrels across
the yard. I got dressed and went over to the kitchen.
Washed myself with the little water dribbling from the
tap. Attached to the handle of the window was a mirror,
with cracked glass. Though it was in two parts, I could
see my face—my beard was growing wildly and was
white! In the lobby I called out, 'Sophie?' No answer. So
I took a banana from the basket and went down to the

yard. The man claiming to be Hansi was standing in the blazing sun, keeping on and on at a dwarf-sized man. I stood in the shade of the wall of the house, watching him. A strange one, this Hansi. But I had to play along with him, if I wanted to survive. I stepped out into the sun. Hansi saw me and came over.

'I need you!' he said.

'Yes?' I bit into the banana. He took me by the arm and led me to beneath the awning, made of leaves, of a wooden hut. I could hear muffled grumbling. Voices. We sat down on two metal barrels that, though in the shade, were so burning hot, I got straight back up again. Hansi remained seated.

'My Grand Vizier is ill,' he said. 'Malaria, typhus, smallpox, hell knows what. People are dying here like flies. Yesterday was the turn of one of my porters. But him I was able to replace. I have to attend the Meeting of the Kings. Without a Grand Vizier, I'm stymied.'

'What's a Meeting of the Kings? And what is a Grand Vizier?' I'd not yet heard about the gatherings of the mighty rulers of the jungle forest. And wasn't understanding a word of this.

'Once a year, the chiefs of the most powerful tribes meet. Have been meeting, for as long as people remember. Different territories take turns to organize it. The location is strictly secret, communicated by messengers who hurry, for months on end, and on jungle forest paths, from one tribal prince to the next. Or by fax if, for once, it's actually working. This time, the meeting is on my territory. Downriver from here, only a stone's throw. What's more, the host can be the last to arrive. The ruler of the upper reaches of Lualaba River, for example, how long do you think it takes him!'

I nodded. The gnome, who until now had been standing, motionless, in the sun, suddenly got moving and went into the shed. He didn't even deign to look at me.

'In the past, the meetings were a matter of life and death,' Hansi continued. 'Nowadays, they're more of a ritual. Demarcation of powers. Social contact too. A bit of vulgar trading on the margins of the conference, even. Although. A few of the kings have very violent fetishes.'

'But you're not a king.'

'You get invited when you've acquired so much power, you can neither be ignored nor killed in an ambush by a few shots. It's a great honour that you cannot dodge. To be invited and *not* go, that would really be the end of you. Well, and then there you are, sitting with the other powerful people. It's an odd feeling at first, right enough. Some have been kings *de père en fils* from the creation of this murderous paradise. Others, like me, are novices. New to power. Your fetishes struggle with theirs. If they make a good job of surviving, the kings, afterwards, can be truly friendly. Otherwise, some have returned home, true, but not lived to see the end of the year. Odd illnesses beset them or they vanished without trace. At the Meeting of the Kings, there are no battles, no scuffles, apart from among the rank and file, if they've been boozing. A year ago, two masters of ceremonies beat each other up, but that's the exception. The kings fight with the glory of their presence, the power of their arguments, their court that impresses the others. With beautiful women. Crocodiles. Stately Grand Viziers.'

He smiled.

'How did you gain acceptance?'

'I deliver the beer.' His smile—though his answer was funny—faded. 'Nothing happens if there's no beer. Beer is part of the ritual. The tribal leaders have it put on the slate. The economic disaster spares hardly anyone. And the two or three who could afford to, don't pay either. Which makes me almost taboo.'

'Have you a tribe then?'

'The brewery staff.'

With a broad sweep of his arm, he pointed at the buildings surrounding us.

'I'm not the only boss of a company who now has the same rights as a long-established king. The managing directors of Toyota and Nestlé Zaire are really important demons nowadays.'

'Mad.' I laughed. 'With you, I'm always sure of a surprise.'

'You said it.' Hansi remained serious. 'I can't go without a Grand Vizier. You'll have to be my Grand Vizier.'

'Don't Grand Viziers have to be black?' I said. I was getting into a sweat.

'Of course.'

'Take one of your men.' I wanted, with a similarly sweeping gesture, to point at them. Dozens had just been working in the yard. Now, though, they'd all disappeared. I dropped my arm. The rumbling in the shed had got louder.

'They're all deployed already. They are my court, every single one of them. I'll be appearing in all my splendour.'

'That doesn't make me any blacker,' I said.

'You'll be wearing a mask. No one will see your face. Besides, we'll blacken it with soot, just in case.'

'But I don't know the rituals. The language! What if someone speaks to me? He'll notice right away that I'm an impostor, and that'll be me—a goner. And you'll join me.'

Hansi shook his head. 'You'll follow, wherever I go, like a silent shadow. Always. And everywhere. You'll take care to look majestic. What's more, they all speak French. They wouldn't understand one another otherwise, that's how different their languages are. Just drop all the consonants.'

'*Oui*,' I said.

He rose, patted me on the shoulder and went into the shed. I followed. I had no choice. I wanted to survive this. The brewery staff were all busy, transforming into demons. Into monster's aides, marshals, court assassins, palm-leaf swayers, king bearers, court oarsmen, cup-bearers. Without further ado, two women undressed me and rubbed soot into my face. I had no hope of fending them off, even if I'd tried. I joked with them a bit, like you do at the doctor's when you don't want to show that, actually, you're slightly worried. But they weren't concerned with me as such. They put me in a heavy costume that stank terribly and scratched my skin. Old billy goat. They hung rags and fetishes on me, dead frogs, chicken claws, snakeskins. Bells were hanging round me like belts. I was soon sweating buckets. I was given a mask, the thing weighed tons, was almost a metre tall, with a tall pointed hat and eyes through which I could hardly see anything more than the legs of the people around me. If I wanted to see their heads, I had to bend far back—and then probably looked like a monster that's afraid that the sky could come crashing down on him. High on my mask, a lamp was attached, covered with a dark cloth. Using a small switch in the sleeve, I could turn it on. Clearly, batteries existed in Hansi's kingdom. Odd demonic symbols became visible.

We left the brewery building and walked—at a measured pace, the rhythm determined by a single drum—down the zigzagging road to the harbour. The other musicians from the court orchestra were carrying their instruments but not playing them—two more bush drums, large sheets of iron that would surely be banged together, rattles and two trumpet-like tubes. We swayed as we walked, all in similar fashion, as though a tiny bit drunk. Perhaps, one or other among us actually was. The drum sounded a bit pitiful. Whether we looked pitiful is less certain. We were over a hundred in number, after all. Over a hundred demons. Right at the front were the space-makers, alert goblins in ferocious masks, who paved the way for us with their sticks and machetes.— That said, there was no one to be seen, far and wide.—There then followed about a dozen tall warriors in serious masks, all identical, all armed with highly modern Kalashnikovs. Next, the brewery army, which was in action all year round, without masks. Behind them, the court orchestra. Then a group of dancers that jumped around wildly, in complete silence, though. Next was Hansi, King Hansi, an impressive sight indeed. He was standing on the shoulders of four giants, their steps coordinated so artistically that Hansi seemed to be floating. There were three giants, to be precise, as one of the four bearers was much smaller than the others. The gnome? Hansi was standing at quite an angle, at any rate. His left hand was holding reins, which were more likely stay ropes; in his right hand was the sword. Over his head was a baldachin, carried by four naked men, their bodies painted blue, who were wearing only blood-red masks and tall, just-as-garish penis gourds. Behind the king was me. I was walking in a dignified fashion, upright, alone. I could see only the feet of the people directly in front of me. But I had a banana-leaf swayer, to provide me with some shade. Right behind me followed a huge colourless box, carried by four men, the only participants in normal working clothes. I had no idea what that was.—At the end of the procession came all kinds of retinue, goats, small lions, a crocodile that had to be dragged along. The women. They were dressed in flamboyant garments, covered in symbols, in embroidered fabrics, *shoowas*, all decorated with the symbols of the clan, the silhouettes of beer bottles. Breathtaking, they looked. Saba, the daughter, at the fore.

'Where's Sophie?' I droned, from behind my mask, once we'd arrived at the harbour and Hansi was on solid ground again. We boarded a whole fleet of dugout canoes, with me—at all times—behind my king.

'On her way,' he answered. His voice sounded hollow too. 'The chiefs' wives never travel with them. They do something secret we're not permitted to know about. No idea what. It's an ancient tradition.'

We sailed, always close to the bank, down the river. We all sat there, looking dignified, as if someone were watching. No one spoke a word. Someone probably *was* watching us, from the jungle forests, all the subjects, in silent awe. It was insanely hot and several times I thought I was about to faint. Hansi was in front of me, positioned there like a statue of a god.

A few hours later, we moored at jetties, built specifically for this event, probably. Silently, we formed our procession and, without a sound, other than the beats of the drum, walked along a broad jungle forest aisle towards a huge clearing full of demons. Wild monsters, terrifying, all motionless and silent. At the centre of the clearing, a stack of logs had been piled. We walked slowly into the circle that the people in masks, sitting around the edge of the clearing, had left free. Like a circus ring. Not a sound, no one stirred, though a thousand people or more were sitting there. Devils. Our tribe was small, tiny, compared to the other crowds of monsters. The bearers stopped so abruptly, I nearly crashed into the gnome. He squealed with fright and said something I didn't catch. Hansi, on his shoulders, must have been swaying fiercely. Appalled, I expected to see him thud into my field of vision. Nothing happened, though. So I raised my mask, let them all think I was afraid of the sky crashing down. Without a doubt, what I was seeing was a welcome ceremony. Hansi, standing proudly on the shoulders of his four men, bowed his head before his rigid, seated colleague, not too much, not too little; and the colleague, after an absolute eternity, did the same—for not too short a time, and not too long. Behind him was his Grand Vizier. Then we stepped to the next one. It took an hour, at least, for us to greet the entire circle and finally get to sit in our allocated area. That is, everyone was seated, except me. I had to continue to stand, right behind my king. He had not told me this, that the Grand Viziers, and *only* the Grand Viziers, had to be upstanding throughout the night of ceremonies. I don't know what kept me on my feet—probably the fear I might faint and fall over and strangers, wanting to be helpful, would undress me (see my presumptuousness!) and kill me. Opposite us sat a king who, and that was terrible enough, looked like Hansi. But. His antipode. That said, his ivory mask, much older no doubt, was losing its hair and already pretty bald. His Grand Vizier and my masquerading seemed similar too. He was standing, like I was. I didn't know, and still don't, whether his face had soot rubbed into it also. More likely not. The sun was low over the trees. We were silent. The air was still. The leaves in the giant trees didn't stir. Before me, in the grass, lay a dead bird.

Suddenly, a low-flying helicopter thundered over our heads, one of those army transporters with two rotors that can hold entire companies. Two more, just as big, followed. They vanished behind the trees, flying lower and lower, and slower and slower. Trails of dust raced across the square and treetops collided with one another. Clearly, the helicopters were landing on a landing field hidden by the trees. The rotors slowed to a halt. We hadn't budged, but the sudden storm was shaking the feathers, amulets and scraps of cloth on our costumes. Even when the horrific episode was long since over, my bells were still ringing. And as the sun was pouring the last of its heat over us, a procession of kings became visible that took my breath away. Not just mine—everyone seemed to turn into stone even more. There were many hundreds of demons, an entire army. Garments that could have been designed by Dior or Versace, or their African counterparts, full, grand, in the wildest colours. The most expensive materials—raw silk, *Crêpe de Chine*, hand-worked lace. The dancers, they alone about a hundred masked people, had large bells whose clappers they held with both hands. Here, too, just the tom-tom of a single drum, a big bass drum banged by a giant in gorilla skins. In the orchestra, spiral-shaped horns, vibraslaps, whistles made from elephant teeth, also Western saxophones, their golden shine. The master of ceremonies looked as if *he* were the king. The real king was dressed in ragged hides and standing on two lions, real spitting creatures, held in check by four tamers with long rods. All kinds of fetish adorned the king. Animal penises, garishly painted testicles, teeth, mushrooms threaded on strings, a red plastic toothbrush too. His clan symbol, visible on all the garments, consisted of fluted lines and seemed somehow familiar to me. A mask that was twice as massive as Hansi's—a lion's head, with blood pouring from the mouth.

He, too, did the obligatory round of welcomes. Bowed his head, briefly, casually. When he reached us, I didn't manage to keep my mask down—I'd only have seen the lions' paws otherwise—and was soon transfixed by the two fierce eyes staring at me through the holes in his mask. Had he spotted my sacrilege? I couldn't take my eyes away. Was trembling. He didn't point at me, though, and mutter a death sentence. Instead, he greeted Hansi with dignity. Hansi too bowed his head, but not too far! The Gothic procession of this very mighty one moved on and finally took its place in the last gap, far away from us. 'The last to arrive again,' a voice snarled behind me. 'Like every year.'—'Shut your gob!' another voice hissed. The sun plunged into the jungle, the trees black silhouettes before the burning horizon. The air turned blue. A wind rose, making the treetops rustle and the savanna grass dance. Birds cried. A monkey jumped, screaming, through a gap in the leaves and immediately vanished. In the distance, the first animal died.

Turmoil suddenly. Two of the men, the only ones not to be looking into the centre of the clearing but into the impenetrable green of the jungle forest, dragged a man diagonally across the square. Naked apart from a loincloth, he kept his head down, and was shaking with fear. I could hear him groaning and recognized him— the stoker from the *Perle des Afriques*. His piece of yarn was ripped and hanging, almost falling off already, from his upper arm. Momentarily, I could see his horrified look. Then the henchmen dragged him away.

Once the night had overpowered the blue of the dusk and I could barely recognize Hansi's masked head bang in front of me, three men lit the stack of logs with torches. There was a burst of flames, sending sparks flying, lighting up the entire clearing and turning the still-motionless monsters into blazing statues. Immediately, however, as if some secret signal had been given, all the musicians in all the orchestras started to play their instruments—so madly, I couldn't tell whether they were playing with or against one another. The dancers, anyway, performed steps that were often repeated. Everyone was singing; the women were the shrillest. Only the kings, their Grand Viziers and the guards remained stationary.

Not one king budged. No one spoke. No one seemed to hear what was going on around him. But the air was quivering, and with it, every king. Something invisible was happening. The fetishes were fighting one another. Lightning flashes, odd streaks of light rather, darted across the clearing, blurring the demons at the opposite edge of the jungle forest. It was as if I were seeing them through fiery water. Screams crashing out of the sky. The dancers' shadows on the wall of the jungle forest—as if Titans were leaping around. Hansi, in front of me, appeared to be floating. He was breathing heavily. Suddenly, his antipode was reeling, keeled over, and had to be supported by his Grand Vizier and the master of ceremonies. His fetish must have taken a bashing. Hansi was back on the ground again. Everyone in the circle gave a moan.

The box at my back flared up. It was a lantern, lit from the inside, decorated with hideous faces of demons, the silhouettes of women dancing and the clan symbol. Elsewhere, too, lanterns suddenly lit up. Not all of them, however. Was an extinct lantern a sign of weakness, or could the ruler in question simply not afford either batteries or candles? I, at any rate, pressed the switch in my sleeve. Now I too had a demon light on my head.

Time no longer existed. I could no longer see or hear anything. Or did so through a glass wall, as if whatever it was didn't concern me. To be a part of this cult would have been too terrible. Everyone around me was getting truly delirious. Was possessed, bewitched. Women were rolling on the ground, screaming, their legs wide apart, while ecstatic men stood over them, thrusting their painted penis gourds to the rhythm of what they were singing. Others were dancing and howling, scratching themselves with sharp sticks till they bled. Yes, the jungle forest itself seemed to dance and frolic. And so I got a veritable fright when, as if at an appointed moment, they all simultaneously stopped. The dancers froze in the wildest contortions. The world stood still, and I could suddenly hear my raging heart. The moment was enough for one of the kings, an inconspicuous one sitting very close to us, to turn to his colleagues with a jovial hand gesture and say, 'A good beer, it wouldn't hurt, right?' His voice boomed.

The dancers and musicians took their masks off and dropped onto the grass. Now, they were laughing and chatting. The kings, too, removed their masks and stood up. To stretch. I needed a piss urgently, pushed my mask up over my forehead like a hat, and went to the edge of the jungle forest. Almost instantly, two other monsters were beside me. I pissed like a horse, concealing my penis with my hand.

'Feels good!' the demon to my left said.

'*Oui*,' I replied, pulling my mask down over my face and heading back to Hansi.

He was sitting between the king who had said the magic word—an elderly gentleman with a friendly face, wearing a costume covered in prepared monkey skulls— and a young ruler dressed entirely in yellow. His garment, his fetishes, his mask—all yellow. All three were shoving pieces of meat into their mouths that their hands lifted from a big, steaming pot. Next to them were three large steins of beer. I sat down behind them, and immediately received my pot and my drink. I was an important man and had my own attendant. She was wearing a skirt with a lace hem and had dusty feet. The kings raised their steins and called out something that sounded like a wild war cry but meant *Cheers*, I suppose. Now I, too, removed my mask and had a drink. It was the Easter bock beer and, I swear, a beer had never tasted so good. My whole face, a lake of sweat, was itching and I rubbed it dry with both sleeves of my costume. Only once I'd finished, did I realize with alarm—what if I'd wiped all the colour away? But my cupbearer, a very young, very black person with a button nose, didn't seem to notice anything. She poured me more beer. I then listened to the kings' conversation. The yellow one had joined another group meanwhile, and Hansi and the king with the monkey skulls—grinning, true, and sounding rather casual—were doing serious business. It was to do with a delivery of Easter bock. Hansi's royal customer wanted to pay only two thousand zaires per litre while Hansi was insisting on five thousand. They met in the middle, of course, and embraced. The king called something over to Hansi and he raised his arms to block the suggestion. But after a few 'But yes! But yes! I invite you!' from his buddy, he got up and both walked off, diagonally across the square.

I, of course, followed them. I was Hansi's Grand Vizier after all and, what's more, would have died of fear if he wasn't near me. I had put my mask back on. The other king's Grand Vizier walked in a dignified fashion beside me, with his mask under his arm. He nudged me, pointed at my head, and so I removed my disguise, clamping it, like him, under my arm. My attendant hadn't noticed anything earlier, and this fellow actually winked at me, like a partner in crime. We ended up outside a large tent; a red light was glowing within. The king lifted the panel that was the door and, with an inviting gesture, pointed inside. Four or five white women were resting on cushions and mattresses, all in black underwear; one had taken off her bra and was wearing red garters. All of them smiled at us.

'Prostitutes from Brussels,' Hansi whispered. 'It's part of the ritual. I can't decline the gift.'

'How could I forget!' the king said, spotting us whispering. 'Of course, your Grand Vizier shouldn't go empty-handed! There are enough ladies to go around.'

'Help me!' I hissed in Hansi's ear.

'Why?' he said. 'This kind of thing is kind of nice!'

'Please!'

I'd have to take my clothes off! My trousers at least, and everyone would see my white bottom! Hansi was now next to his friend again, his mouth up to his ear. He was telling him a longish story. 'Oh!' he chuckled. 'I get it!' His Grand Vizier, listening in shamelessly, burst out laughing. 'There's no helping you there, boy!' the king said, entering the tent with Hansi. 'Have a beer on me!' The Grand Vizier disappeared inside too. Before he lowered the door panel behind him, he turned around and poked the middle finger of his right hand through a ring he formed using the thumb and forefinger of his left.

I nodded. When I couldn't hear anything, anything at all, I took a step towards the door of the tent. I probably wanted to lift it and peep in. But my gaze fell on something odd on the ground, tangled up in trampled grass. I lifted it and found myself holding the unfortunate stoker's piece of yarn. Now he no longer had an amulet to protect him! Getting the scent of something, like a fox, I went around the outside of the tent and immediately spotted a messed-up bundle of something lying, about fifty metres away, outside another tent near the edge of the jungle forest. I scurried over. The stoker was tied up and half-unconscious.

'Hey!' I whispered, slapping him on the cheek. 'I'm a friend of yours.'

He opened his eyes. 'Psst!' he whispered back. 'They're in there!' And indeed, at that very moment, someone in the tent started to speak, in a language of the Congo, and so terribly close that I jumped back. All my bells started ringing. We listened carefully, not even breathing, but the voice continued, undeterred.

Thank God, one of the amulets sewn onto my costume was a Swiss Army knife. I ripped it off and cut through the stoker's fetters. His lower lip was bleeding. But he could walk. We crept to the edge of the jungle forest. There, I handed him his piece of yarn.

'Your amulet,' I whispered. 'You now need a lot of luck.'

'It's a fetish,' he answered just as quietly. 'Which didn't help my grandfather any before me. He'd worked for the white people, at the Falls, and when he couldn't take it any more they stood back and watched him starve to death.'

He disappeared without a sound into the blackness of the jungle forest. In the tent, his guards were laughing loudly at some joke or other. I saw to it that I vanished. Halfway between the edge of the jungle forest and the brothel tent—there wasn't a bush I could've hidden behind, nothing—an armed troop was coming directly towards me, doing what was nothing less than a goose-step. At the centre of the troop, the only one not in step, walked the very powerful lion-ruler, now without his mask. He was no longer a young man, a heavyweight Colossus, and was wearing horn-rimmed glasses. I'd stopped, stock-still, like a rabbit caught in the headlights. The tight horde did indeed seem to want to flatten me and stopped right in front of me only because the foremost bodyguard, a giant like his master, raised his hand. He stared at me in hostile fashion. In his other hand was a huge truncheon.

'What is it?' the lion-ruler asked from behind him.

'A Grand Vizier, Your Excellency,' the giant answered, not taking his eyes off me. 'And he hasn't thrown himself to the ground.'

The lion-ruler became visible among his guards. He was now wearing a kind of toga with jagged lines on it, his clan symbol. This was the end, I knew. A white man here, at the most sacred place of black power, and he'd not kissed the hem of the magnificent one, even.

'I can trample all over you,' he said. 'I can let you live. I can do whatever I want. Whose Grand Vizier are you?'

'Anselme Kisangani,' I stammered.

'Your bad luck.' His look froze even more. 'Hansi's brewery is on my tribe's territory. I will repatriate him soon. Very soon. Back to the Reich, as you say. He's a false hyena, your Hansi.'

'He's my best friend,' I whispered. 'He took my wife from me.'

The king stared at me. Then began to laugh. Upon a signal from the commanding giant, all the others laughed too. The king raised a hand and the whole pack fell silent.

'I like you!' he exclaimed. 'You're different some-how!' He rummaged in the folds of his garments and produced a business card that he pressed into my hand. 'If you ever have any problems, call me. My secret number, that is. *Priorité absolue*, you understand? No one else has it, not even him there.' He pointed at the commander of his gang of thugs who was staring at me, his eyes popping out of their sockets, as if he were a golfer about to play his final shot and I was his ball. 'And to think he's *my* best friend.'

He pointed at my right hand. Only now did I notice it was clutching the stoker's piece of yarn. 'Your fetish?'

I nodded.

'Yarn is first rate.' He had a piece in his hand too, albeit a brand-new piece of golden yarn. 'So that's why. I was wondering why I didn't feel like having you whipped to death.'

He returned to his place in the marching formation. It was written all over his friend's face that the latter yearned to kill me—so before he could I sprang off into the dark night. The bunch of them started moving again and marched across to the brothel tent.

Four of the gorillas went in and, almost immediately, Hansi and his royal friend came racing out, both head first, naked and with an erection, each glans a shining red. They fell among the beer bottles and dishes. The lion king didn't deign to look at them and stepped into the tent. I saw how he took his glasses off just before the door panel closed behind him. Hansi and the king picked themselves up. I ran over to them.

'Another two or three thrusts,' grumbled the king. 'And I'd have reached the point—'

The door of the tent opened again and a fluttering bundle flew out. Their clothes. With them flew the

Grand Vizier, my colleague, whom the bodyguards of the very powerful ruler must have overlooked initially. He didn't have his trousers on either. He landed right at my feet. I held out my hand and helped him to his feet. '*Merci*, my friend!' he said. 'I think I'll get mine cut off too.'

Hansi had pushed his lower jaw out so far, his lower lip was way ahead of the upper one. His eyes were staring into far distances, and in the middle of his brow was a deep furrow. This face—this was how Hansi had looked as a boy when he was raging and it was better not to speak to him. This, too, he'd learnt from my Hansi. He went off, with his clothes under his arm, in the direction of the still-seething fire. Even the cheeks of his bottom looked furious.

Wherever you looked were lying sleeping demons and women in witches' costumes, tangled up in one another, their mouths open, snoring. A young woman— her garment covered in leopard paws—had her thumb in her mouth. Hansi's master of ceremonies was lying in a puddle of beer next to his overturned stein. Completely exhausted, I lay down beside him. I didn't care whether anyone saw my skin. I fell asleep immediately.

*

The sun wakened me. The master of ceremonies had gone. Instead, Saba lay not far from me, in the arms of a man. She opened her eyes. 'Hello,' I said, and she smiled without recognizing me. I wanted to explain to her who I was, why I was so covered in soot, but at that moment the master of ceremonies squeezed in between us. He had a camera up at his eye, a highly modern Minolta, and was photographing me. '*Parfait!*' he said when I tried to smile. He pressed the button once more, then vanished among the men and women who, all around, were struggling to their feet. The clearing, in the light of the new day, had lost all its mystery, all its dignity, and looked more like one of those refugee camps we know from TV. Everyone was getting their bits and pieces together. Hansi was already awake too and wakening one of his Kalashnikov soldiers with a kick. His lower jaw still looked like a drawer. Roaring, he urged us on like a malicious staff sergeant, and so I too hastened along behind the brewery clan that, curiously, wasn't rushing to the river where we'd left our canoes but to a large car park hidden behind some bushes. Buses, jeeps and trucks were parked close to one another and being boarded by excited men and women. Everywhere, the dust of tyre tracks, and immediately I knew where the lion king got his clan symbol from—from the profile of Michelin X tyres.

The whole fleet of cars belonging to Anselme Kisangani was waiting with their engines running— three Berliet trucks with open load areas, the corrugated-iron Citroen, with the canoes moored on its roof, and a very dirty R4. We jumped on as they were already moving off. I ended up in the R4, beside Hansi, who drove. Behind us, Saba and two of her girlfriends were giggling, with no regard for Hansi's bad mood. I now understood the hurry he was in. For our convoy managed to be the first to reach a narrow dirt road leading into the jungle, just ahead of a three-wheel Vespa to which about ten blacks were clinging, and an oxcart full of women that had set off especially early. Branches hit off the bodywork as we plunged into the jungle. Behind us, the Citroen that the trucks were following. Hansi went up into fourth gear, pulled his lower jaw in and tried to laugh. It still sounded bitter, but he was on the way up again. Monkeys, moving wildly, fled before the vehicle.

'So,' I shouted above the engine noise, 'did you win?'

'We're all still alive anyhow.' He closed his eyes as the R4 shot into a wall of vine and crushed its way through. 'And I sold ten thousand litres of beer.'

'I can imagine who the strongest was. Him with the lions.'

'Has been for twenty-nine years!' Hansi drove so quickly through a hollow full of stones that the underbody broke open. 'He has fetishes you haven't got a hope in hell against.'

The jungle forest was steaming such that Hansi had to turn the wipers on. Green, a dull, more and more moist green. If I looked up at a sharp angle, I could sense the light of the sun. No animals. Just once, in black mud, the tracks of hippos or elephants, when we came to a ford that Hansi tore through without slowing any. Water sprayed over the roof and the engine started to drown. But we arrived safely on the other side and howled our way up an embankment. From the wing mirror fluttered a vine.

'When I didn't want to join you with the prostitutes,' I shouted, 'what did you tell the king?'

'That I'd cut your dick off.' Hansi was roaring too. 'I couldn't think of anything better.'

For quite a while, we drove in silence. The dirt road, covered in car tracks, led to a savanna. Dazzling light again now. Yellow, almost head-high grass sprawled all over the roadway. The grass was swooshed away beneath us. Here and there were individual trees with crowns like roofs. And under them, zebras. We were rattled all over the place so much, the chatter of the women stopped too.

'Do you remember?' I said. For a moment, I was seeing the black chief sitting beside me as the real Hansi; I noticed my mistake, but continued anyway. 'When I was four, and you five? We were looking at the photo album. A photo of me, Harry Harder and my mother!'

This, he couldn't know! This, he couldn't have learned by torturing Hansi or using witchcraft. But he said without hesitation, 'And the dog! Like it was today!'

'You tore the photo out of the album and took it over to Anselm!'

'Me? *I* did?' For the first time, Hansi took his foot off the gas. He looked at me. '*You* took the photo. *You* took it over to Anselm. He gave *you* a pop-gun for it. Not me.'

I could remember the gun. It was just . . . I thought I'd got it from my papa. I could push the bolt—to which I attached a rubber stopper—into the barrel and when I pulled the trigger, a spring would fire it some ten metres. With a bit of luck, it would stick. I shot at everything, at the door of the house, at cats, at the scarecrows and, once, even at the red face of Herr Harder. The bolt, on that occasion, did indeed stick—to the middle of his brow. Harry Harder, kindness in person otherwise, roared as if I'd just tried to murder him. 'Me?' I said. The terrible Hansi beside me nodded. I felt dizzy.

We were now driving in the jungle forest again, on a wide, dusty track. Potholes. Once, we passed a Simca, from the fifties. Signs of civilization too: telephone wires, hanging loosely from trees; lemonade cans; once, a wrecked car overrun with green stuff. Only as we were pulling into the brewery did I find my tongue again.

'I need an answer for Anselm. Why aren't you sending him any more money?'

We stopped and got out. The three friends in the back headed for the house. Hansi was standing on the other side of the radiator bonnet, and blinking. In the dazzling light of the sun, he now looked very black.

'I wanted *him* to come here. Him, not you.'

'He'd never have survived the climate here.'

'No.'

We went into the house too, washed in the kitchen as best we could, and took a seat at the table. We drank some beer. Above us, on the ceiling, the fan was turning, cooling us down. The room was pleasantly gloomy. Beyond the open door, the day was burning. Far off, very far off, in rooms I didn't know, the women were laughing.

Hansi pushed a piece of paper across to me, a sheet of A4 containing a short typewritten text. 'Give that to Anselm. Tell him to sign it.' I took the piece of paper and realized I couldn't read the text as my glasses were broken. I put it, unread, in my trouser pocket. Hansi lifted his beer glass and drank it empty. Out in the yard, barrels were rolling again. The Stanley Falls were roaring too.

The master of ceremonies, now a brewer again, came into the room and put the Minolta down in front of Hansi. He had something for me too, though, a yellow envelope on which was written in felt-tip—in such big letters, I could read them—*A ouvrir avant l'atterrissage à Zurich*. He raised his hand in salute and vanished. I put the envelope away too.

'Your plane's waiting outside,' said Hansi.

'Who is waiting?'

'I have a delivery for Kinshasa. Five thousand litres of beer. The owner of one of these diamond fields is having a party this evening. Eight hundred guests. A Big Band from Chicago. If you want to spare yourself a return journey on the *Perle*, you'd better board. Now.'

I got up. Sweat was cascading down my body, I was maybe going to get out of here alive! My bag was soon packed. Hansi accompanied me to a nearby runway in the jungle forest, where a twin-engined plane was waiting. An original version of the JU 52. Or a prototype of the DC-3 that had never gone into production. I shook Hansi's hand.

'Make sure Anselm signs the piece of paper before he reads it,' he said. 'Before he realizes the significance of it, at least.'

I nodded. 'I'll post it to you.'

'You'll bring it to me in person.'

'If you want.' I nodded again. 'I'll bring it back.' But if I got out of this hell, I vowed to myself, I'd never return. Ever again.

The pilot let the plane roll a little, to make me get a move on. At that moment, I saw Sophie. She was walking across the airfield from the jungle forest with a machete in her hand that she was using as a stick. She looked like a missionary who, enlightened by her black faith, was returning from an evangelical tour. Her face was dirty and radiant. From her belt were hanging an aluminium drinking bottle, a compass and something that looked like the scalp of a heathen she'd slain.

I ran towards her. 'I have to get that plane,' I panted, standing before her. 'All the best, Sophie.'

'You're looking great!' she exclaimed, beaming at me and kissing me. 'Splendid!'

'You are too.'

'Take care!' She gave me a gentle push. 'I'll never see you again.'

I headed over to the open hatch of the plane. As I climbed the little ladder, I realized she'd followed me. I looked down at her.

'I wanted to tell you one more thing,' she called out, competing with the noise of the propellers. 'Back then, my father gave all the dogs the same names as us. The first was named after Mama. When it died, he was in complete despair. The second dog was given my brother's name. When it died, my father was out of his mind. He got odder and odder, started talking to himself, and to me as if I were his wife. The third dog was called Sophie, of course. That day, I caught him putting poison in Sophie's food. He looked at me with blazing eyes. He'd killed the other dogs too. He was mad. I *had* to get away. Either with you or with Hansi.'

The hatch closed behind me and we started to move. I could see her through a window. She was standing, her hair blowing in the turbulence caused by the plane accelerating for take-off. She waved. We took off. When we curved around, she came back into my field of vision. She was walking with Hansi, back to the brewery, hand in hand. We were gaining in height. The Stanley Falls were spraying, white, completely silent, surrounded by the green jungle forest. Then we got up into the clouds and I sat on my travel bag.

Three hours later we were in Kinshasa. And indeed, a Swissair plane was leaving that same evening for Zurich. Why, actually, had Anselm booked the outgoing flight via Brussels? At Customs, the same officer. He was clean-shaven, wearing my sunglasses and didn't deign to look at me. An MD-II. With a moan, I sank into a seat in its Business Class. I was just about the only passenger, and spoilt good and proper by the stewardesses. Orange juice, champagne, a superb meal. I read the headlines of the most recent newspapers. All over the world, people were still killing one another. But the weather in Zurich was promising to be mild. An Indian summer almost, though August was far from over. While we were still flying in sunshine, night—below me—was creeping over Africa. At some point—without my glasses, so writing without seeing what I was doing—I completed my expenses for Anselm on a piece of paper I got from the stewardess. Hotel, the ship ticket, the taxis. Then I went to the toilet. As I washed my hands and looked in the mirror, I saw I had a full beard. White. Tight curls. And that my face was a deep black.

*

In sheer panic, I sat in my seat, clearly so perturbed, the stewardess came up and asked if she could do anything to help. Initially, I shook my head. Then I asked for some schnapps. I felt a bit better after that. I was black! I was as black as Sophie and Hansi! I almost tore open my shirt until some skin became visible—also black. My hands—still pink on the inside only. My calves when I rolled up my trouser legs—ebony. I didn't dare to unbutton my trousers and look at my dick.

Of course, I slept badly. Dozed off, woke again with a start as wild monsters were dancing in my dreams. Two intermediate stops, in the middle of the night in the outback. When day broke again, I tried to get going by having a coffee. But I'd have needed real coffee, two double espressos, and not this watery stuff. Then I remembered the envelope. *To be opened before landing in Zurich.* Indeed, we were flying over the Alps already, their snowy peaks glowing in the morning light. I tore the envelope open, and soon had a green something in my hand, a passport of the Republic of Zaire, the imposing coat of arms which I could see despite not having glasses. True, I couldn't read in whose name the document had been issued, but it had to be mine as I recognized the photo. It was the one the master of ceremonies had taken. I smiled. So I'd been black then already! The transformation must have taken place at some point during the monster night!—Even a visa had been stamped into the passport. That it might be a residence permit, was something I couldn't hope for. A tourist visa rather, I supposed, valid for three months. How much must Hansi have paid for this document, which looked so genuine because it *was* genuine?

At the airport in Zurich I walked with all the other passengers along the never-ending corridors. There were indeed very many now. An elderly official flicked through my passport page by page and typed my name into the manhunt database. Which name?

'*Parlez-vous français?*' he said, eventually, in a kind of French.

'*Oui.*'

'What is the reason for your trip to Switzerland?' He continued to speak French.

'Tourism,' I said.

When he began to flick through the passport again and checked the visa a second time, I added, 'My father lives in Switzerland.' I was glad *he*'d chosen the language for our negotiations—French—and that I wasn't forcing him to wonder how come I could speak such good Swiss German. 'He's old.' And when that still didn't stop him from staring into my travel document—'He's on his deathbed.'

'In Switzerland?'

'Black people die everywhere,' I said.

He looked at me, then nodded and gave me back the passport. I went through the Baggage Reclaim hall where my fellow travellers were waiting at a conveyor belt that was just starting to move. The first thing it spat out was a surfboard in a case. Behind the door that said 'Nothing to declare' was nobody at all, and so I could go, unfrisked, through the last sliding door separating me from free Switzerland, behind which many people were waiting for their loved ones. All white. I pushed my way through them, got into a taxi and was taken to Anselm's place. In Witikon, crop fields, tall yellow stalks. A warm sun that lacked, however, the power of the African summer. We turned into a familiar street. A lot of green. Everything as it had been, everything quite different. I gave the driver a huge tip, and he gave me a receipt.

As I walked up the flagstone path to the door of the house, a man came towards me. He ran past so close, we touched. Nonetheless, I was unable to see his face as he had a grey crate on his shoulders. On it, the symbols of the Wehrmacht. He couldn't see me either, and was cursing loudly to himself. More an old man, not a young man.

Anselm was standing in the open doorway, as if he'd expected me. He was wearing a dressing gown that looked like the one back in the day, and under it, striped pyjamas. His bare feet were in leather slippers. He looked even more wasted than when I'd departed, and didn't seem to see me either.

'It's me,' I said, 'Maybe you remember my voice?'

He woke up and examined me. 'You've been sent by Hansi?'

'Yes.'

'Why didn't Kuno come?'

Without entering a discussion about my identity, I went into the house. 'What's going on today?' Anselm said, behind me. 'Henner leaves and a negro arrives.' I'd not set foot on his property for about fifty years, yet I found my way around instantly. The full-length mirror with the gold frame was still in the hall. As I examined myself—I was seeing the full length of my body for the first time—Anselm pushed his way into the reflection. He was as white as chalk, raised his arms helplessly, and dropped them. I, on the other hand, was impressive. A sturdy African. Hair like that of a steel brush, broad lips, big white eyes. The beard, oh well. I bared my teeth, winked at the laterally reversed Anselm, and went into the lounge. In the same old places, the familiar wingback chairs or their similar successors. I sat down in one. Before me, on the wall, was still the ancestral portrait, a fat and much younger Anselm, with a ruff around his neck and a hop in his hand. All around the room, the

Louis- or Empire-style chairs, the gold of which had dulled. The piano, however, had vanished.

'This was once a racially pure house,' said Anselm, who had walked much more slowly than me and yet was out of breath. 'My remark, of course, is not directed against you, sir. I am simply observing. Times have changed.'

Though he looked as if he hadn't slept since my departure, he was standing bolt upright. All bearing, with red eyes, though. As if he could read the silent question I was thinking—'What's wrong with you?'— he said, 'My adjutant has left me. Just now, it was. My home help.' He gulped and stood up even straighter.

'Let's deal with the expenses first.' I didn't want even to begin to hear about his worries and took out the piece of paper. I couldn't read it, true, but knew the amount. 'Five hundred and twelve francs. Almost nothing for an African trip. Check it.'

I placed the details of my expenses and his black leather wallet with the remaining dollars on the low table between us. He signed without checking the arithmetic, and while still standing. His hand was trembling and he wanted just one thing—to get rid of me as soon as possible. That said, when I gave him Hansi's letter— 'From Hansi. Could you sign it, please!'—he did begin to look for his glasses after all. First patted the outside of his dressing gown pocket, then checked the surface of the table and bent down to look under the chair, then found them in his dressing gown after all. 'Henner had been my general dogsbody since Tobruk,' he said, unfolding Hansi's document. 'The invasion, the Battle of the Ardennes, the fall of Berlin—all those things, we got through together. Always fanatically proper, my Henner. Ill, not once. And just today he realized that he could never stand me.'

He read the document. Then said, '*These* are your expenses. Four hundred and seventy francs. How come you asked for five hundred and twelve?'

'The taxi.' I pushed the receipt across the table.

He added it to the envelope and put the envelope away in his dressing gown. 'So what did I sign just now in that case?'

I didn't know either and took the piece of paper out. He read it, read and read, read it again from the top, his face getting redder and redder. He started to sweat, finally was dripping with sweat and roared, 'That's outrageous! Outrageous is what this is!' His eyes were popping out of their sockets, his cheeks paled—paled beneath the fiery red—and he was gasping. Next thing, he was reaching for his chest, breathing another sigh, and crashing to the floor. He lay there, on his back, his arms out, his mouth open. He was dead.

I bent down, took his glasses from his nose and could finally also read what Hansi had sent him through me. Anselm was staring up at me as if expecting an explanation.

Dear Hansi—the letter began, typed on a typewriter with a broken *r*—*I am now old. Death is near. And so, with these lines, my will and testimony, I want to tell you that I have never forgotten what I promised you in 1957 when you left for the Congo—that you will be my successor. I know that you have never forgotten this promise either. Not for one day. And I know that only this certainty helped you persevere in the deadly Congo. Now is the time. My dear Hansi. You are the legacy that Aline, who loved us both so much, commended to me. I am therefore bequeathing to you my breweries, my fortune and my house in Witikon. The thought that you and your Sophie will live here comforts me. Signed, Anselm Schmirhahn, 8 August 1994.*

Beneath it, a little wobbly, but unmistakable, was Anselm's signature. The document had a postscript which read, *PS: You agree, no doubt, that the Kisangani branch will be in good hands if entrusted to Kuno. Brief him in the necessary. His future will be black or non-existent.*

I put the odd document away. *Today* was the eighth of August! Hansi had predated it! Anselm was still looking at me, and I bent down and closed his eyes. 'Yes! Yes!' I heard myself say. Though I felt no guilt in the matter, I took a handkerchief and wiped the arms of the chairs and the door handles. I was a black man. When I closed the door of the house behind me, I realized poor Anselm hadn't had the time to give me the five hundred francs he owed me. Instead, I still had his glasses in my hand. I stepped out on the street. Not a soul. Our house, at the edge of the forest, looked—with its closed shutters—as if it had gone blind. The flowers in the garden were growing wild and needed watering. I walked off quickly, down the steep road to the bus stop.

*

When I got to the old people's home, the bell of the church in Fluntern was striking ten. I climbed up to the first floor without meeting a soul. The emergency light above the door to my father's room was flashing, and I started to run. Sister Anne turned up at the other end of the corridor at that same moment. She got to the door before me, opened it, shouted something into the room, switched the emergency light off and closed the door again. She then stood, staring at me. Her lips were trembling and her eyes, like big round plates.

'What's wrong with him?' I said.

'He does that a few times a day,' she replied. 'He'll do anything it takes to lure me to his room. Not even the emergency button is sacred.'

'Oh.'

She continued to look at me, a look I'd never seen on her before. In her eyes was a deep, no, absolute seriousness. She was examining my face as if a secret was concealed behind my brow on which her life depended. She was breathing so violently, it sounded like a groan. Then she whispered, 'What's your name, sir?'

'Kuno.'

'Kuno!' She seemed to have found her voice again. 'We have a carer who is also called Kuno. Quite nice, but unreliable. He's been gone for a week, just vanished, and I have to do his work in addition to my own. Cantankerous old people like him in there.—Where are you from?'

'Congo. I've just landed.'

She nodded and looked down her body. She looked wonderful, in her nurse's uniform that, again, was unbuttoned at the front all the way down to the last two buttons above her stomach. This time, her slip was white. Her hair was let down over her shoulders, blonder than ever. Her feet, of course, were in Zoccolis. Bare toes, the nails painted red. And her eyes, her blue eyes had got even bigger. Her lips were shaking now. She reached for my hand. 'And me? What do you think of me?' she whispered.

'You know already,' I said. 'I love you.'

She turned a deep red, as if I'd spilled paint over her. For a moment she stood there motionless, almost without breathing, as if she were taking an irreversible decision. Then she nodded—the answer to the question she'd put to herself—opened the door to the room of Herr Andermatten and pulled me in. Inside, she flung her arms around my neck and kissed me.

How was I to resist? Then, though, I did say, 'This is Herr Andermatten's room,' or rather, I tried to—her lips were pressed to mine still. 'If he turns up, we'll be shown the door.' I sounded like someone trying to speak with a gag on. 'This very day.'

'Herr Andermatten is dead.' Sister Anne removed her lips from mine and put them to my right ear. 'He had some kind of tiff with the other Kuno.' She was whispering and I could feel her warm breath. 'Ran into the manager's office, began to say, "Herr Kuno—" and dropped dead. We'll never know what my colleague Kuno did. A good deed, in any case.'

We were now lying on the bed and kissing, and started taking the heavens of love by storm so eagerly, we probably missed out on this one or that. We found ourselves in seventh heaven so soon, at any rate, we didn't know any more who was white and who was black. It was overwhelming. Then, having returned to earth, we lay next to each other. Looked at each other.

I'd never seen Sister Anne—Anne now! The days of Sister were gone!—like this before, so serious and so naked.

'I've waited all my life for this moment,' she said.

'Me too. Since I first met you, good lady.'

'Good lady?' She smiled.

'Since I first met you, *Anne*.'

'That's not so very long ago.'

'It's longer than you think.'

Out in the corridor, voices were whispering. Twenty of them, at least. They were muttering, hissing and got downright loud until fierce Psst!-s quietened them down again. 'That's Sister Anne!' Frau Zmutt—who was deaf—roared. 'But who is the man?' Her question fanned the would-be secret whispers like a blast of air reaching a fire.

'I better go straight out.' Anne reached for her slip and put it on. 'They'll wait at the door until the Day of Judgement otherwise.'

I was faster than her, tore the door open and jumped—the way the black god made me—out into the corridor. 'Rrrrr!' I roared, banging my chest with both fists.

'A negro!' Frau Zmutt shrieked. 'A naked negro!'

The old people scattered. Herr Zwahlen got such a shock, he bashed Frau Zmutt—ahead of him on her way back to her room—against the wall of the corridor. Herr Börlin, otherwise the gentlest of gentlemen, stumbled and shouted at Frau Gross. Doors banged shut, keys turned in their locks. Herr Jeanneret was the last to disappear. He had Parkinson's, walked with a Zimmer, had a room at the end of the corridor, and was pushing his way there slowly—and yet in the greatest of hurries. He groaned. Finally, he'd made it too, and the corridor was so empty again, you'd have thought no one had ever set foot in it. A deep peace. Above my father's door, the emergency light was flashing.

I ran back to Anne who was buttoning up her uniform, put on my shirt, got—running already—into my trousers and entered my father's room without knocking. He was lying motionless on the bed, staring up at the ceiling and breathing in short bursts. His skin was yellow, almost transparent. His lips had vanished into the cavity of his mouth.

'Papa!' I said.

He looked at me with feeble eyes. 'I am not your father, sir,' he muttered. 'My son doesn't have a beard.'

'You need a doctor!'

Anne opened the door. She'd buttoned her uniform up the wrong way and her hair was all tangled.

'Get the doctor!' I said.

She nodded and disappeared again. When I turned back to my father, he had closed his eyes. I bent over him and could hear his irregular breathing. His pulse was weak. 'Papa,' I whispered. 'Papa!' But he couldn't hear me. So I went over to the washbasin, lathered up and shaved using the old-fashioned razor he'd been using for thirty years. A deep-black face was looking out of the mirror at me. A man of about fifty-six with tight grey curls and thick lips, whom I didn't recognize.

'Papa?'

This time, he heard me. 'Oh there you are, Kuno,' he whispered without opening his eyes. 'Who was the negro with the beard?'

'No one,' I said.

'I'm dying.' He paused to draw breath. 'I'd like to be buried in my forest. Behind the house. Not in one of these awful cemeteries.'

'About the photo,' I said. '*I* am to blame for Mama being murdered. *I* took it from the album.'

'I can tell you who's to blame,' he whispered. 'The one to blame is—' His mouth remained open. He was no longer breathing.

The doctor came in. He was as burly as ever, greeted me in a business-like manner, so in no way astonished, took my father's lower arm, let it drop, and shone a tiny torch into his eyes. He looked at the clock. 'Ten fifty-eight,' he said. 'The extinction of the candle of life. Time of death.' He noted his findings.

I left the room. I stood in the corridor for a while, not knowing where to go next. I then knocked on Herr Berger's door and, when there was no answer, opened it. Herr Berger was lying motionless on his bed too, and had closed his eyes. No breathing, at least none that I could hear.

'Oh no!' I said. 'Not him too!'

Herr Berger jumped up. 'Who are you?' he said, sitting up on the bed and examining me with panicked eyes. 'Death?'

'Kuno,' I said.

'Death is black.' He exhaled noisily and swung his legs out of the bed. 'But you are not Death.' He rose with difficulty, his legs still trembling. 'Death has a scythe. Or a sting. Depending. Sometimes both. You gave me quite a fright.' He was even smiling now, having regained his self-control. 'And you're not Kuno either. Kuno was the carer, here on the first floor. Nice, but thick as a brick. Since he's been gone, Sister Anne has been doing this floor. A stunner of a woman. You can't imagine how many times I've pressed the emergency button already to see her.'

'Your friend is dead,' I said. 'Kuno Sr.'

'That can't be,' he said firmly. 'Just yesterday he said to me he had to hold off dying until his son came back. He had something to say to him.'

'What?'

'He'd found out who was to be blamed for his mother's death.'

'Who?' I said. My heart was thumping.

'The murderer, of course! Who else? You perhaps?'

The phone rang, out in the corridor. Herr Berger darted out, as always, but I lifted the receiver before him. A woman's quiet voice. She asked was Herr Berger there.

'For you,' I said, holding the receiver out to him.

He took it and listened into it. Gulped, and his whole body—not just his legs like before—started to tremble. I pushed a chair towards him that he sat down on. He was sweating.

'It's you,' he said.

He listened again for a while, without a word. He just nodded, once, twice. The woman at the other end of the line seemed to have a lot to tell him.

'The room next to mine has just become free,' he said. 'You're a lucky devil.'

He hung up.

'My wife,' he said. 'For the first time ever, I wasn't the first to get to the phone. She's eighty-one now. She's been released from the clinic. Cured.'

'That's wonderful,' I said.

'She's on her way here. Right now.'

'Even better.'

He sighed. 'Why do you think I always put on a voice when I answered the phone?' He answered his own question. 'To be able to say, "Herr Berger, no, you must be mistaken, there's no Herr Berger here." I didn't want to see her again. It had been too terrible. Her crying. Her face. The way she walked around the house as if from another planet.' Tears were glistening in his eyes. 'All those years, I was paying for the treatment, the cure. On the first of next month, I'd have been bankrupt. Good timing on her part, somehow or other.' He blew his nose.

'You'll get on famously,' I said. 'Like Philemon and Baucis. First, though, we have to bury your friend.'

Anne helped me to get my father onto a bier while Herr Berger looked on, shocked, at his dead friend. We covered him with a sheet. Then we rolled him along the corridor, into the lift, through the side entrance to the car park, where we loaded him into the VW Transporter in which he'd come to us a whole eleven days before.

Herr Berger got in first and sat beside the bier. I was at the wheel, Anne beside me. As we were turning out the gate, Cindy was coming towards us. She was wearing her Hard Rock Cafe T-shirt and holding the baseball player's hand. She looked, puzzled, at the familiar bus and its unfamiliar driver. I waved.

On our journey to Witikon, no one said a word. A lot of traffic. Our street, that said, was as empty as ever. I parked outside Anselm's house, which looked cold and uninhabited. The three of us heaved the bier up the garden path, snorting and cursing, as the wheels had been constructed for hospital corridors and not gravel paths. Several times, the whole carriage threatened to topple over.

By the time we got to the top, Anne and Herr Berger were red in the face and I was bathed in sweat, at the very least. I fetched a spade and a shovel from the shed. The forest floor was soft, thank God, and half an hour or even an hour later, I'd dug out a hole big enough for my dead father. We tried to lower him as gently as possible into his grave. He slipped out of our hands, though. The sheet shifted and a yellow hand became visible. Herr Berger was holding the hand-carved Général Guisan and threw it into the grave. 'That's all in the past now.' I then quickly shovelled all the earth back. A small burial mound resulted, on which Anne placed dahlias, phlox and larkspur that were growing wild in the garden. No one said a prayer, we didn't know any. 'Let's go,' I said after a while.

On the way back down, the bier was faster than us and I had to run to keep it under control. Anselm's house was as silent as a pharaoh's tomb. We didn't speak on the way back either. I left the VW Transporter in the car park. We entered the building, as dirty and sweaty as three participants in an expedition that they never expected to survive. At the bottom of the stairs, I stopped, held my hand out to Herr Berger and said, 'Take care, sir!'

'I liked Kuno,' he said. 'But I still have Sister Anne, at least.'

'I wouldn't count on that too much,' she said. 'Today was my last day at work.' She kissed him on both cheeks. He turned a deep red, almost as much as Anne herself a few hours earlier. 'Adieu.'

We watched him as he went up the stairs slowly, an old man in an old suit. With each step he took, he looked more elegant. More worldly. At the top, he turned to us and waved. He'd now returned to being the cheerful gentleman who enjoyed having the travails of manhood behind him. He vanished from view.

I showered in Anne's room. It was packed full of African masks, sculptures, rugs. A veritable collection, and a good one. She saw me looking and said, 'Africa has always inspired me. Too bad, I'm not black.'

'You can't have everything,' I said.

Then we set off. Anne was carrying a bag that had space for not much more than her toothbrush. On the driveway, we encountered an old lady, a puckish creature, in a skirt made of colourful patches, who was waving madly, but not to us—for when we turned around we saw Herr Berger at the main entrance. He was wearing his hat now and, hesitantly, raised a hand. Then they both started running. They met halfway and fell into each other's arms. Looked at each other for a long time, not letting go. Finally, they entered the building, with a heavy duffle bag between them that Frau Berger must have been dragging all along, but which I noticed only now.

At the airport, I bought two tickets for Kinshasa. I still had the five hundred francs from Anselm, of course, and Anne had brought along what was left of her last wage. 'Do you have visas for Zaire?' the hostess issuing the tickets asked. Before Anne could answer, I did. 'But of course!' Anne looked at me and I nodded.

I then exchanged the remaining money into dollars, with the exception of some that I kept aside to buy sunglasses—the same style as the last one—and a razor. From a payphone, I called my father's GP, who was no doubt also Anselm's. True, he wasn't the only doctor in Witikon, not any more. But he was the only one for people who had lived for sixty years in this sprawling suburb that, in their youth, had been a village. The receptionist answered.

'This is Anselm Schmirhahn,' I whispered, imitating his guild-member cadences. 'I don't feel well. Please come quickly.' I groaned hard and hung up.

We went through passport control and to Gate A86 where the familiar MD-II was waiting, ready to fly back. Different stewardesses, otherwise exactly like last time. I even had the same seat which I let Anne have so she could be at the window and look down at Africa.

*

It was still chilly when, in the light of the rising sun, we strolled across the apron of Kinshasa airport to the Customs shed. I put my new sunglasses on. Once again, the same officer was behind the metal-topped table and, this time too, he was wearing my sunglasses. He stared at me. Then took Anne's passport and started flicking through it as slowly as if he were a classicist and the document, full of hieroglyphics.

'What is the purpose of your visit to the Republic of Zaire?' he finally muttered in French after all.

'She's my wife,' I said. 'And the visa's in here.' I pushed my detective novel towards him, the same one as last time. He took it, read the title, said, 'It's not up to much. Just telling you,' opened it and cast a quick glance at the dollar notes inside. He didn't as much as blink. 'This is the visa,' he said. 'And where are the marriage documents?'

I took the book back, inserted the last of my dollars and handed it back to him. He nodded. 'This is a forbidden import!' he said loudly for the benefit of the other passengers, putting the book in the drawer. To me, he said, 'Nice glasses you've on.' I nodded. '*My* favourite authors are Diderot and Ambler,' I said. He looked at me as if searching his brain for the echo of my sentence, then turned, with a reluctant wave, to the next passenger, a fat black man wearing a dark red fez.

Outside, the chilly air had turned into early heat. Anne was beaming; this was the way she liked it. I was just starting to palaver with the taxi drivers—among them the one from last time—when, far back on the airfield, I spotted the plane in which I'd flown here the day before yesterday. Its engines were running and men were in the process of pushing away the steps. 'Let's go!' I said, grabbing Anne by the hand. Waving our arms, we ran up to the plane that was beginning to move already. It braked, the ladder was relowered and we climbed it. The hatch fell shut behind us.

'Hansi told me to wait for you,' the pilot called over his shoulder to me. 'But I thought you weren't coming.'

'Customs,' I roared. 'Always gives you hassle.'

The engines roared. The plane droned as if it wanted to split apart on the spot. Just before the end of the runway, we took off. The sea in the distance, the Livingstone Falls looking colossal even from the high, and then there was only jungle forest below, it too a sea, green waves as far as the horizon.

In Kisangani, the sun was showing no mercy whatsoever as it burned in the sky. Anne was no longer beaming, but gasping for air when we stood on the bumpy patch of grass that passed as the airfield. I put an arm around her, then took it away as I, too, was drenched in sweat. Fortunately we didn't have far to go. A few minutes later, we were in the brewery grounds and climbing the steps of the ochre-coloured house.

I knocked and entered.

Hansi was sitting at the table, in the same tropical clothing he'd worn when he set out, back in the day, for Africa. Yes, it was Hansi. It had to be him. I was also Kuno, after all. I didn't recognize him however. Grey eyes, thick lips, his face all wrinkles. He'd not managed to button up his jacket, two buttons were still undone over his stomach. The helmet lay in front of him, and beside his chair was a suitcase. Above him, the fan was turning. 'Oh there you are,' he said.

'May I introduce Anne?'

Something or other caused me to be formal. 'Anne, this is Hansi.' Anne smiled through the streams of sweat running down her face and Hansi, infected by me, bowed vaguely but without getting up. He pointed at two empty seats and we sat down.

'Had you any problems?'

'No.' I gave him the will. 'That is to say, Anselm is dead.'

He cast a glance at the rather tattered document. 'I'll go now in that case,' he said. 'The plane merely turns here. Sophie likes the *Perle des Afriques*. I don't.'

I pointed at a tub of water—in it, quite a lot of bottles of Easter bock. 'We're dying of thirst.' I opened three bottles, and he did in fact remain seated and took one. He looked at Anne. 'Drink, madame. It'll do you good.' The corners of his mouth rose, almost as if he were smiling.

'I've never needed a beer more,' said Anne.

'That's how I see it too.' His smile was now so clear that, in anyone else, it would have qualified as uninhibited laughter.

We had the beer. It tasted delicious, and I opened three more bottles. We knocked those down in a oner too. Hansi then stood up, decisively and energetically. 'From now on, you're the boss here,' he told me. 'I have instructed everyone. You won't have any difficulties. Don't forget the next Meeting of the Kings. You're now a king-monster.' He took his suitcase, nodded to us, went over to the door, opened it and turned back. 'Oh yes. I almost forgot.'

'Yes?' I was just opening two more bottles.

'The very mighty lion king, the one with the fetishes no one has a chance against, has given me an ultimatum. He claims the land the brewery is on is his. The time runs out this evening. I reckon he'll attack you tonight.'

'What?'

'You've twenty-two Kalashnikovs.' He smiled. 'Won't be a problem.'

I gulped and Anne looked inquiringly at me. She hadn't understood what this was all about, or only half-understood. 'What's his name actually?' I said. 'This horror of a ruler?'

'Don't you know?'

'How would I?'

'It's better that way.'

He closed the door and went down the stairs. Through the window, I could see him crossing the square. Sophie stepped out of the shade of a pile of barrels. She too had the dress on that she'd worn back in the day, and just one sandal. The other was in her hand. She was dangling it like a handbag, and limping along a few steps behind him. I didn't recognize her either, though I was sure it was my Sophie I was watching. Where had her little chin gone, her little nose? Hansi put an arm around her and waited until she'd put the second sandal on. Both laughed. The dog shot out of a doorway and, barking, jumped up at them. All three vanished behind Saba's accounts office.

Anne and I remained at the table. We looked at each other, held hands, kissed across the table and drank one beer after another. It was too hot to do anything else, and the heat—the beer too, increasingly—stopped me from thinking about the coming night. About the fact that by morning, we'd be skewered on adjacent stakes, with no ears, no noses and mutilated genitals. Anne was drinking one beer after another and I was perhaps out-drinking her. The square of light the sun was casting through the window wandered across the floor. The fan was humming. At one point, in the distance, a monkey that had woken too early screamed. Beer barrels rumbled across the yard and the Stanley Falls, of course, were roaring.

At some point, the sun started to turn the table and the bottles red. The room was glowing. Anne, too, looked different from before. More beautiful, more radiant. Her hair was no longer blond and straight but now flaming purple and curling. Her lips had become fuller. Her skin was darker. Yes, I was actually able to watch her turning black. I couldn't take my eyes off her as, completely aware, she put another bottle up to her mouth. Two days, it had taken, in my case. Perhaps, with women, it happened faster.

When Anne was finally black (she looked stunning), I could hear distant drumming. As if the horizons were dancing. It was coming closer, this rhythmical droning, and was soon pretty loud. It surrounded us on all sides.

Anne could hear it too and looked up, as if to ask what it was. 'They want to kill us,' I said, not at all afraid, oddly. On the contrary, a wave of a very new feeling washed over me. Hot, splendid. As if I'd been awaiting such danger for decades.

I looked at Anne, to see if she was frightened. She was, but for a different reason, for she'd taken out her vanity mirror—to check her lipstick, I suppose—and seen what had happened to her. She stared at her reflection.

'My God,' she murmured. 'My God.' She didn't sound panicked, like I'd been in the plane toilet, but surprised, and when she said, 'My God!' for the third time, her voice sounded delighted. 'Have you seen this?'

She jumped up, came running around the table, pulled me up out of my seat and fell into my arms. Her mouth was open, her eyes ablaze, her teeth shining. 'A miracle!' she exclaimed. She was sobbing and laughing, and I followed her lead. We were clinging to each other, also because, now that we were standing, we realized we were drunk.

The door was pushed open and Saba came rushing in. Behind her, the man came panting up the stairs with whom she'd lain the morning after the demons' meeting. This time, she was wearing a shirt and jeans and clutching a Kalashnikov. 'They're here!' she said. The man behind her nodded vigorously. The drums were indeed so loud, they might have been down in the yard.

'Didn't you go too, madame?' I said, trying to stand independently. 'Back to Switzerland?'

'My country is here!' She raised her head, like a queen. 'And my man too.' She took his hand. He tried to smile but when the sound of the drums outside swelled to what was veritable chaos, he groaned and looked to and fro, fearfully, between her and me.

'What will we do now?' I asked Saba.

'That's what I wanted to ask *you*. Hansi said you're the boss now.'

'Okay.' I leant on the edge of the table to steady myself. 'I'll assume command. I order you to organize the defence.'

'There are at least three hundred of them,' Saba said. 'Machine guns, mortars, hand grenades. Everything.'

'I have a fetish.' I took the piece of yarn from my pocket. 'It coped once before with the terrible lion king.'

Saba took it, reverently, like you would touch something sacred. She was trembling. 'It is—it's real,' she whispered. Her man, too, looked at the piece of yarn, amazed.

'You can keep it,' I said, 'I have another one. An even better one.'

She tied the yarn around her neck. 'Yarn fetishes are the best of all,' she said. 'The real ones are one hundred and more years old.'

We went down the external stairs. It was dark now and the only light, apart from a pale moon, was coming from large barrels in which oil was burning. There were some on the roofs of the storage sheds too, casting their light as far as the jungle, which was screeching and raging as if the trees themselves had gone mad. Hysterical little drums and big heavy drums. Shrill horns. Bells that rattled more than they rang. And women, screaming, like they were anticipating the outcome for us.

Outside the shed where I'd been transformed into a demon, my entire army was standing. The soldiers were holding their weapons and looking at us, perturbed. Saba said something to them I didn't understand—pointing at the yarn around her neck—and they ran off, shouting, each in a different direction. I stopped the last of them and took his Kalashnikov. 'I am appointing you our messenger,' I said. 'You'll run to and fro between Saba and me.'

He nodded and took up position behind Saba.

'And what will we do?' I asked her.

'You two secure the east side.' She pointed at the roof of a particularly long storage shed. 'It's very possible that they'll attack from there.' She spoke clearly and assertively, as if she'd always had the authority to give commands.

Anne and I dug ourselves in behind a low wall that ran along the roof. We were overlooking a harvested cornfield behind which the jungle reared. Two barrels were burning in it and lighting the black wall of trees. Shadows were dancing. The noise was never-ending. Every now and then, a burst of gunfire from a machine gun. A nervous soldier, one of ours probably, shooting at the invisible jungle forest ghosts. My eyes were closing but I opened them right away. The jungle was spinning around me, or I was whirling in it. Trees, shadows, the barrel-lights—I was seeing them all double. I groaned and took deep breaths, in and out, in a bid to see the phantoms over in the jungle forest but without their doppelgängers. At one point, I also shot into the jungle forest, without hitting it maybe. I put an arm around Anne and realized she was sleeping. Her mouth was open, she was breathing quietly, and lying there, smiling. I kissed her. Then, doubly attentive, I stared across at the jungle forest, was still staring when my eyes had long since closed for I was dreaming I was wide awake and looking unwaveringly into the jungle forest that wanted to kill us.

When I woke it was bright as day. The cornfield lay empty and still in the dazzling sunlight. The stubble cast little shadows. The barrels were black. The jungle forest, a green wall. Not a sound to be heard. Apart from Anne, lying on her stomach beside me, snoring gently.

I scratched my head. What was going on? Had I simply drunk too much beer and imagined gory cannibals who wanted to get their hands on us? Had I been having nightmares? I got up, yawned, stretched my arms and spat down onto the cornfield.

A few hundred Kalashnikovs started to shoot, the bullets whizzing past my head. One, very close. I threw myself down behind the little wall and—terrified— cursed to myself.

Anne was awake and staring uncomprehendingly at her right forefinger. It was bleeding. A ricochet had grazed it.

Now Saba's soldiers were shooting madly too. Or, I assumed it was them. I couldn't see anyone, not in the jungle forest and not on the roofs. Mud sprayed in the cornfield. Yellow stubble flew through the air, and in the jungle forest branches were wavering. It sounded as if we'd all gone mad, all at the same time. I rummaged in my trouser pockets for a kerchief I could use to bandage Anne's wound. Nothing. Instead, I found myself holding a piece of card, a business card, on which in gold embossed letters, reminiscent of Roman temples, a single word was written: MOBUTU. Beneath it, in scrawly handwriting, a phone number written in pencil. 5-1-1-1-2. I gasped for breath. When I'd said to Saba yesterday that I had another fetish, a better one even, I'd just been talking nonsense. The optimism of drunkards. But I did have one. And this was it.

I climbed, as fast as I possibly could, down the steep ladder to the inner courtyard where the messenger came running up to me, screaming that Madame Saba had sent him, soon we'd have no ammunition left, and we had not the slightest hope.

'Ten minutes,' I said, running across the yard. 'You've got to hold out for another ten minutes.'

He saluted and ran off.

I rushed into Hansi's house, which was now mine, and immediately found the phone. It was still lying next to the sink. I dialled the number. Hissing, rattling and cracking sounds. A distant satellite high up in the universe was struggling with a receiving station on earth. Then someone lifted the receiver.

'Yes?'

'This is Kuno speaking,' I said. 'Hansi's Grand Vizier. You gave me your card with your *Priorité absolue* number.'

'But of course!' Mobutu exclaimed. He sounded pleased, and as if on a different planet. 'What brings you to me then?'

'Your army is in the process of killing all of us. No doubt, this is happening without your knowledge and against your will.'

'I like you,' said Mobutu. 'But I don't like Hansi. Sadly, my people will only stop once they get him. Dead or alive.'

'He has left Zaire and will never return.' I drew myself up, regally almost, though I was alone in my kitchen. 'I'm not his Grand Vizier any more. I am his successor.'

The other end of the line was quiet and I was afraid the connection had been lost.

Then, though, the mighty lion ruler spoke again.

'You must visit me some time,' he said. 'I'm building a ceremonial room in order to be able to receive foreign dignitaries. Old friends. Bush, you know, Mitterrand, or you. The room will be big enough to hold Saint Peter's Basilica.'

'Thank you,' I said. 'But what are we going to do right now about your soldiers? They're shooting my brewery to bits.'

'That is happening against my will. Without my knowledge. As you surely realize. Put the commanding general on. I want to speak to him.'

I put the phone down on a silver plate lying in the sink, took a dish towel from a hook—white, more or less—and left the room. 'Cease fire!' I shouted to the messenger who, with panic in his face, was coming running again already. 'Now it's the turn of *my* fetish.'

He stared at the phone glistening on the plate and rushed back to Saba. Waving the white flag, I walked diagonally across the cornfield I'd seen from my lookout during the night. Anne was probably watching me. The stubble made dignified walking impossible, but I made every effort. In the middle of the field, I stopped. Waited, motionless, with the flag in one hand and the phone in the other.

A few minutes later, a man came out of the jungle forest. He was wearing modern combat dress and had hung his regalia over it—feathers, skulls, lions' tails. In one hand he had a Kalashnikov. He was walking in as dignified a fashion as I had done, obstructed just as often by the stubble. He was the commander of the guards, the giant, and looked now, too, like a murderer. A few paces away from me, he stopped.

'A call,' I said. 'For you.'

He took the receiver and held it to his ear. 'Yes?' He sounded just like his master but the look in his eyes was significantly more sovereign. That said, he suddenly folded as if someone had kicked him at the back of his knee. He bowed to me, again and again. Finally, he removed the receiver from his ear. 'The most mighty of all the glorious is gracious enough to place my fate in your hands,' he said with a voice that was already dead.

I took the receiver. 'Yes, what can I do for you?'

'I told him that he's ready for the crocodiles.' Mobutu seemed to be in a very good mood. 'But you decide.'

'Your best friend,' I said. 'That would be such a shame.'

'You're right there. Over and out.' Mobutu hung up and the line went dead.

The general seemed still very perturbed. 'If I'd realized,' he murmured, 'that you are under his personal protection . . . '

'I didn't realize myself,' I said, rolling up my white flag and putting the phone in my pocket.

He spun around and ran back across the cornfield. He stumbled several times and almost fell. Then disappeared into the trees. Next thing, I heard were barked commands, shouts, curses, the rustle of vines through which mortars and artillery were being dragged. The army was leaving. The soldiers were no longer in any way quiet, they were chatting and laughing. Their voices sounded more and more distant, just like the single drum that was beating a quick marching rhythm. Soon, it was only the monkeys, the birds, the wild cats and the Stanley Falls that could be heard.

On the roofs of the brewery, my soldiers were standing and dancing, their guns over their heads. They were singing and shouting with glee and shooting into the air. Among them, arm in arm, Saba and Anne. They looked so similar, they could have been taken for each other, two black beauties. When I entered the yard, they were climbing down the ladder. With them, Saba's man. Saba had taken her shirt off—making the piece of yarn seemed whiter still against her black skin—and Anne had bandaged her finger with a red rag.

'How did you manage that?' she said.

'Saba managed that,' I replied. 'Her fetish.'

Saba nodded.

'There's something else,' she said.

'What?'

'Bébé.' She pointed at the man.

'He needs work.'

I looked at him. He was gigantic, a mountain of a man, black. He seemed to be nothing but strength. 'Can you brew beer?'

'No,' said Bébé.

'I take it you can roll barrels though?'

'I'd guess so.'

'He studied microbiology,' Saba said. 'At the Sorbonne. The highest final grade in his year.'

Bébé raised his arms as if to apologize. 'Not a profitable profession,' he murmured. 'In Kisangani, at least.'

'I am appointing you as my Grand Vizier,' I said.

'Thank you.' He looked at Saba. 'I hope I can do it.'

'Hey listen,' she said, pointing at me with her chin. 'If *that one* was able to, you can.'

*

I'm living meanwhile beneath the equator as if I've never been anywhere else. A native. Day after day, the air is so glowing hot I get up before the sun and, when it's at its peak, try to doze off for a few hours. I go around almost naked, loincloth, short trousers, that kind of thing. A hat when I have to be outside. I now speak nothing but French and can speak a broken form of the natives' language.

Anne and I are more in love than ever. We sleep in Sophie and Hansi's bed. Eat at their table, from their plates, even their favourite meals that the cook prepares for us with the same enthusiasm as he used to for them. I am—have been for a year and seven days now—still speechless when I catch sight of Anne. I never tire of looking at her shiny white eyes and teeth, her lips, tight curls, her breasts, the black stomach around which she always wears a string of tiny wooden beads. She, conversely, loves me just as much. I am at least as black as her after all. We kiss night after night. By day, we work.

With Saba, Anne is computerizing our book-keeping. It took a bit of a fuss to get our Macintosh. But we have it now. As well as the laptop and the printer. We've also got a self-contained power supply for when, as happens a few times every day, the electricity grid crashes. Not a solar system—that, I would find too expensive and it would never get here in one piece—but an old-fashioned generator, powered by two waterwheels in the river deep below us. I've done a proper brewer's apprenticeship and can now produce beer. African beer, in theory at least. I was in all the different departments, learnt how to start the mash and calculate profitability, and I rolled barrels across the yard. Bébé did exactly the same and is my right-hand man.

I've managed to increase production of Easter bock by eighteen per cent. We even export it, to the tourist centres in Senegal and along the Ivory Coast as well as to specialist shops in Amsterdam, Brussels and Zurich. For six months now, we've been brewing lager beer completely without hops and malt. The amount included had become symbolic in any case, and importing the ingredients, complicated and expensive. We use a herb called k'hama—it grows wild here—and so the beer tastes totally bizarre to the European palate. That said, there aren't any European palates here. We are—in the heart of Africa—the market leader. The only brewery, far and wide. The likes of Heineken or Tuborg that manage a sixty-per-cent market share down on the coast, you can only get here at the bar in the Intercontinental, a pauperized version of the Intercontinental in Kinshasa, a bar I've been in only once and where I drank two

Heinekens. No customers other than me. A melancholy barman, dusting bottles of liquor that hadn't emptied any in months. A motionless fan on the counter, because the air conditioning no longer worked. Dismantled, stolen, resold. By the barman, I suppose. The foreign beer already tasted unusual to me. I'd got used to my own.

I've started collecting all the money owed to Hansi by the tribal princes—the bills that were still unpaid. About half the powerful rulers actually paid up! Even Mobutu sent a cheque, signed by his bookkeeper with his fingerprint. That said, he—and only he knows why— deducted ten per cent. His 'discount'. Our cash flow, Saba says, has never been so good. At any rate, not while she's been doing the books.

The town, Kisangani, has about three hundred thousand inhabitants after all—I see only when I go out of the gate of the brewery and keep going, way ahead, until I reach the first bend on that zigzagging road down. The town then lies far below me. A chaos of houses. The clay roofs of the old dwellings and huts with corrugated roofs, some squeezed in between high-rises, the walls of which are full of cracks, the windows smashed. A forest of TV aerials. A stinking haze over all the streets. I was down there a single time, when I drank the Heineken as I mentioned. I suddenly longed for all the ado in a city.

In order not to be recognized—the police persecute the representatives of the former power of the tribes and, though they have no support whatsoever among the population, can be pretty aggravating—we set off in simple loincloths. The whole court, albeit without the women. We were an army of grinning, somewhat fearful men. Only Bébé couldn't be persuaded not to wear the Grand Vizier's lion fetish—so, the sacred paws dangled rather randomly over his hairy chest. We roamed—with no one paying us any attention—through the glowing hot streets. Bars, bazaars, stalls full of junk. The roar of the Falls was much louder down there than up where we were. It drowned out the shouts and chat of the people swarming about. Baskets on the heads of the women, cursing men dragging around cratefuls of coconuts or bananas. Fleeing pigs with children on their tails. A few cyclists. Here and there, a bus engulfed in black clouds of diesel fumes, a bus that the passengers clung to. People calling, laughing, shouting. At one point, carnage outside a restaurant, a fight, only seconds it took, by the end of which one of the fighters, still a boy, was on the ground bleeding. No one tried to help him, we didn't either. We ended up in a cinema, if not the one we'd actually been looking for. We'd left the map behind, up at the brewery. So we ended up in a shack made of wooden planks and cloth, and saw not the film we'd planned—*Out of Africa*—but *Rocky III* in which, in a boxing match, with life at stake, Sylvester Stallone, an Italian in trousers made from an American flag, insulted a Germanic hulk in French—the film was dubbed—and, when the latter barked something back in German, knocked him out. Without a word. My men howled with pleasure. Before the end, I stepped outside and, at a bar beneath a banana-leaf roof, drank sweet lemonade. I was soon joined by Bébé who wasn't enjoying the film either. As for the others—no idea what they were up to after we'd left. At any rate, suddenly three police cars pulled up, lorries with metal cages at the rear, and we had to watch as the whole brewery workforce was led away. The men were talking all at once to the policemen who, bored, hit their truncheons against the palms of their hands. The workers didn't get home until the next morning. Two had black eyes and one, a sprained arm. At dusk, Bébé and I crept past houses and huts, in all of which the same TV programme was being watched, a soap opera about the forest demons in old times. Once home, we drank another bock beer in the kitchen, and when Anne and Saba joined us, we told them about all the things that had been going on in the streets of the town—but not about our cinema visit and the police coming.

I also attended—as I was now a very mighty one myself—the annual Meeting of the Kings. This time it took place way up in Lualaba, near Ntala. It's just been. We sailed upstream in eight giant dugouts, taking almost three weeks as our outboard engines kept breaking down. I was wearing Hansi's mask which was even heavier than it looked, and—when we entered the circle of the clans—I stood on the shoulders of my giants, the fourth of whom—the gnome—had recovered. His substitute last year, had retaken his original role as the triangle player in the orchestra, and seemed to have forgiven me. At any rate, he gave me a friendly grin, quite unlike last time. Bébé was my Grand Vizier. He was dignity personified, stood motionless behind me throughout the ceremony and accompanied me without the slightest murmur of protest to the brothel tent when I was invited by the same, very relaxed, ruler. Or, rather, the latter apologized to me so profusely—for, naturally, not being able to invite me to join him, because of my terrible handicap—that, to my own amazement, I informed him I'd been cured. Everything was in the best working order again. He beamed and clapped me on the shoulders. I was given—he distributed his gifts with the look of a connoisseur which he no doubt also was—a woman of about forty, from Charleroi, called Claire. Broad hips, fat thighs, breasts like cushions—but the most disconcerting thing was her white skin. She looked almost ill. She sensed my irritation and was all the more intimate with me. Gasping, next to me, was Bébé.

The ceremony went well in other ways too. Like Hansi, I won my battle of the fetishes against my antipode. I'd thought it was all a ritual, shadow-boxing, including—and above all—the motionless struggle with my distant opposite. That monster beyond the blazing flames that looked exactly like me. But I could soon feel that the battle was draining me out—so much so that, in the end, I was about to collapse and faint. I couldn't breathe and was seeing stars. At that moment, my opponent fell over. His men took care of him, comforted him until, still floundering, he could retake his seat. A broken man. My lamp lit up again and his remained dark. Next came the beer drinking—this time Mobutu asked the ritual question, a faux pas clearly, as the muttering of the other chiefs near me was unmistakable— the food, the chats, the casual trading.—Only the all-in-yellow ruler was missing. I asked my new friend, the one from the brothel, what had happened to him. 'He's dead,' he said. 'He wanted to seize the town. Came to a terrible end. Battered to death like a dog. With him, the whole of his court. Even the crocodiles. *Quel con!*'

For the return journey, though sailing downstream, we needed almost two weeks. One dugout capsized and a woman drowned. We looked for her for hours, without success. When we finally arrived home, completely exhausted, Anne was already back long since. More beautiful than ever, refreshed, invigorated. I asked her what she'd been up to—what the women's custom involved. She just smiled.

The jungle forest—what dominates everything is the jungle forest, though. It's everywhere, it surrounds you. It's silent and yet full of voices you can't make out. Human beings? Animals? Ghosts? It is motionless and, whether or not you are on the watch, gets closer and closer to you. Unstoppably so. If you don't defend yourself—and even if you do—it will overgrow you, sooner or later. You will not escape it. It's been there since the beginning of time, and it will be there when the likes of you no longer exist. It watches all you do—not indifferently, no—but it has time on its side. Revenge is not unknown to it, the death cries from within it are the proof. But it is patient. It's not jealous if a different form of death sorts you out sooner—a sudden malaria, being bitten by an animal that descends from the sky, the axe of a native who has gone mad in the heat. It sees you at all times, it never sleeps. A few million eyes of its infinitely many lizards are always open, the shimmering leaves are them blinking. Where its mouth is, you don't know. It will snatch you. That is so certain, it doesn't matter whether or not you watch out.

The jungle forest arouses me like nothing else. Every evening, when the sun is no longer burning so cruelly and Bébé comes to supervise the night shift, I plunge into this paradisal hell. Call it a deadly Eden. Take one step past the first tree trunks and you're in a different world. Sounds that you've never heard before, some so close, you jump back, appalled. Other distant laments, shouts of celebration. A constant roaring that might be the echo of the Big Bang. Snakes dangling from trees hiss in your face. If they bite you, you're dead. Cats spit at you and take off. From leaves the size of roofs drip erosive poisons. The light is gloomy. Blue. As if you were walking on a sea floor. Crane your neck as you will—no sky. Hardly any hint of a sun. Leaves, branches, climbers, creepers. Soaring tree trunks covered in moss. Lichens that, if you try to touch them, sweep off up the tree because, actually, they're netlike spiders. Any contact with your skin and you'll scream in pain. Flowers with gigantic blossoms, all blue, though in daylight they're all kinds of colours.

At one point, the jungle forest gets steep. A wall of clay and moss, full of roots as thick as tree trunks that make climbing possible. Don't slip on the damp wood, don't fall off, or you'll smash to pieces among the dead tree trunks far below. Up on the crest of the hill, like the pointed pinnacle of a mountain almost, stands a single giant tree, towering over the others. Its branches have grown so evenly, I can use it as a ladder. In the crown of the giant tree, I've built a hut, a proper house. A table, a seat. A view you wouldn't believe. You've never seen the like. Below you, the green jungle forest, steaming in the heat, as far as all the horizons, and no doubt far beyond. As if it were embracing the globe. At similar heights in the distance are similar tree monsters, like signals. The green is constantly changing—no wonder, the language of the natives has thirty-four words for it. When the sun plunges into the jungle forest, it glows. A flaming fire, beautiful, terrifying. The trees then turn blue. Now it's too late to go home. Anne almost died of fear the first time I stayed in the jungle forest because I was watching the blazing trees too long. Now, because I'm writing, I stay awake at night too. I sit in the light of a butane gas lamp. Other nights, I strap myself to the trunk so as not to crash into the depths while asleep, and not to be allured by the singing and drumming either that reaches my ears from all around. As my eyes begin to close, I see—in the distance, where the horizon blurs into the sky and the sun, unlike here, leaves some last light—the glittering golden roofs of Timbuktu or the tents of the Tuareg in the Sahara. Tiny triangles. Alexandria, its pillars. The Mediterranean. And, hard to believe, occasionally the white peaks of the Alps.

For seven days, I've been sitting here with no sleep. Without eating. Or drinking. Millions of flies are buzzing around me. I've now typed 2,93,848 characters. It's no small matter; trying to catch up with a present—for which my life needed fifty-six years—in seven days.

I want to enjoy it when I get there. Now! Now, I am writing and being at the same time. I do indeed shout

out in celebration, and while I cheer I am noting that I'm doing it. Ah! If those people in Zurich could see me now. The late Herr Andermatten, for example. Or Frau Zmutt.

Over. Past. What I write from this moment on *will be*. If what will be, will be. If the snakes, the big cats and the madman's axe don't get in the way. At first light, I will untie myself from my tree, climb down the mountain, slog my way through the jungle forest, step out into the open, rush through the yard, run up the stairs. Gingerly open the bedroom door and peep in. Anne, my Anne, will be lying on the bed, hidden under mosquito nets, only her feet showing. Black feet. Motionless.